Praise for
Sloan Parker's Other Books

"…I have loved every one of Sloan Parker's books and this one is no different. …exciting, suspenseful and most importantly, romantic. The love story between Walter and Kevin is so sweet and real. They have a connection that can't be denied by either one of them."
—*Literary Nook on HOW TO SAVE A LIFE*

"…a smoothly flowing plot that has enough angst, obstacles, and mystery to keep you glued from the first page to the last... I thoroughly enjoyed reading this fascinating and enthralling book and would definitely recommend it to anyone looking for a fantastic read that is worth every minute spent on it."
— *Trish at Mrs. Condit Reads Books on HOW TO SAVE A LIFE*

"…a beautiful love story ... You can't help but fall in love with Linc and Jay. I can't recommend it enough. I can't wait to read more books by this author."
—*Caroline at Book Lovers Inc. on BREATHE*

"…an incredibly poignant story where the emotions are profoundly moving, the characterization is perfect, and the suspense is riveting."
— *Nannette at Joyfully Reviewed on BREATHE*

"…an emotional and sensual blockbuster."
—*Joyfully Reviewed on MORE*

"I loved both of the heroes... and found myself easily rallying for their relationship to grow from being best friends to developing a loving, romantic relationship together that lived long within my heart long after the story was over."
—*Night Owl Reviews on TAKE ME HOME*

More Than Just a Good Book
A Novel

SLOAN PARKER

A NOTE TO READERS

MORE THAN JUST A GOOD BOOK was originally written as a short story and was then expanded into a serial novel made available via my newsletter and website. (The original short story is chapter one of this novel.) I started the project as both a thank-you to my readers and a way for me to try out writing, revising, and editing a novel in parts instead of working on it as a whole. I wrote the individual installments as time allowed while continuing to work on other projects. This resulted in a bit longer delay between installments than I'd originally hoped, but I wanted to give this story as much attention as I do all my other novels. To all of you who followed along during the writing of this story, thank you! Your excitement and encouragement made this project all the more special for me. I had a wonderful time creating Scott and Mark's story, and I hope you enjoy the final result.

Much love and happiness,
Sloan Parker

Chapter One

"What the hell are you doin'?"

Scott stopped reading and tilted his head back. Boy, the guy standing next to his chair sure was tall. Huge. And not happy. Mad, really. Enraged.

"Uh...reading."

"Readin' here?" the gigantor asked.

What was the big deal? "Yeah. It's the library."

"You're in my seat, you little shit. Get up." Gigantor gripped Scott's neck with a huge hand and hauled him out of the seat. "Read somewhere else, nerd. This here's where I take a nap." The lug shoved Scott aside and plopped into the plush upholstered chair.

Scott stumbled but caught himself before he fell. There were five other people in the stacks nearby, and every one of them stared at him. Most of them laughed. It wasn't anything that hadn't happened to him before.

Pissed, but not pissed enough to take on a jerk that big, he skulked off in search of another place to sit, clutching his backpack and the comic he'd been reading. The first week of his last semester in college, and some jock the size of a boulder makes him feel like the biggest loser on campus.

He wouldn't let it ruin his good mood, though. He'd just purchased a copy of the new *Red Arch-rival* comic book. Time to do a little reading before hitting the paper for his Advanced Economics class.

Scott settled in at a table, the toes of his sneakers tucked behind the bottom rung of the chair, opened the book, and immersed himself in the story again. He'd just gotten to the part where Red was about to learn the identity of the hidden infiltrator who'd blown the planet Xano's weather controller when the huge bald jerk had thrown him out of the chair.

He got two panels in again, and then Gigantor's gruff voice rang out. "I'm not movin'."

Scott peeked over the top of the comic. Another man stood next to the chair he'd vacated. Dark brown hair and darker eyes. He wore tan slacks and a white long-sleeve dress shirt with a splash of red zigzagging across a black tie. The pants hung off the curve of his ass in a way no dress pants had ever looked on Scott. The man was lean, but even through the clothes, the curved muscles of his arms and legs and that fine ass were hard to ignore. Scott was so entranced by said ass, he almost missed the gorgeous man's reply to Gigantor.

"I'm not asking you to move. You need to leave the library." His arms were folded in front of him as he glared at Gigantor.

"Why?"

"Because you're harassing other students. Students who are here to study."

"That kid?"

Uh-oh. Gigantor was pointing at Scott.

"He wasn't studyin'. He was readin' some fairy comic book. Kick his ass out."

Oh no. Scott could *not* get kicked out of the library. He *lived* in the library. Between studying and the stack of new books he read each week, he'd never make it. Books cost too much for him to buy enough for how much he read. And he had four roommates at his apartment. Where would he do his homework? It was never quiet enough for reading, let alone studying. He was on his way to graduate school. He had to keep a 3.98 GPA for the scholarship.

"No," the dark-haired man said, his voice stern, unapologetic. "I'm kicking you out."

Scott sucked in a sharp breath. The man worked at the library and talked like that? Scott loved a man who liked books, was smart, and had strength to him—someone who could show Scott a little dominance in bed, control his body, make him fly apart with need and pleasure. Not that he'd ever had anyone in bed with him who fit such a perfect description, but it didn't keep him from hungering for it.

Gigantor stood, towering over the other man. "Don't you know who I am?"

"Yeah. And you're still kicked out. It doesn't matter what position you play on the football team."

Gigantor's arms twitched; his biceps flexed.

Scott flinched from where he sat. He hid behind the comic book again.

The dark-haired man didn't move an inch. He was going to get a serious pounding. All because Scott had to move. Was there a library policy stating you couldn't steal another man's seat? Should he tell them he didn't mind moving? Save the man from the impending torture Gigantor was sure to inflict? But Gigantor didn't raise a hand. He snorted and strode past, shoving the dark-haired man with his shoulder on his way by.

Scott dropped the comic. He scooped it up again before anyone saw him sitting there with his mouth gaping.

No one stood up to someone Gigantor's size. It was kinda scary and neat and...sexy as hell. Scott's blood ran south, his hardening cock begging for a touch. Good thing he was sitting. He hadn't had such an immediate attraction to anyone before. Not someone he hadn't talked to yet.

Not that he spent a lot of time talking to men. He kept to himself, read, studied, and read more. It wasn't like he was a virgin, but he'd learned a long time back the men he wanted didn't want him.

But the man he was lusting after was looking right at him. And walking toward him.

"You okay?"

Scott swallowed around the lump in his throat. The man's voice sounded better up close. Low, confident. The deep tone zipped through Scott. If only he could shove his hand down his pants, grab his cock, and pump his hips, push the swollen flesh through his fist until the relief he craved shot out of him.

He breathed deep. Arousal and the scent of the dark-haired man overpowered him, made him dizzy. Irresistible. Clean. With a hint of a spicy cologne. It wasn't helping Scott with what to say to him. All he came up with was *please take me to bed.* "Uh, uh-huh" was what he managed.

"That jerk is such an ass. He never does anything but sleep."

"You work here?" Better. A coherent sentence.

He smiled at Scott and laughed. The laugh sounded like a purr.

Scott was already counting the number of fantasies he'd be able to use when he jerked off, all of them starring this man. It would be enough to last him through midterms, maybe finals. It wasn't like he'd have any actual sex before then. He didn't mean to be celibate. He'd get laid all the time if he had his choice in the matter.

Maybe this man would want him.

There he went again, thinking about fantasies as if they could be real. He'd have to settle for jerking off and using his favorite dildo while he imagined the dark-haired man slamming into him, taking him right there against the fiction shelves, his own bare cock pressed against the novels of Stephen King and Dean Koontz.

Damn, he'd have to use that one as soon as he got home.

MARK COULDN'T HELP but laugh at the blond-haired man staring up at him. The university library was huge and there were a lot of employees, but how the hell had the other man not seen him? Mark had worked at the library for the past four years.

But he was seeing Mark now, looking at him like he was the main course at an all-you-can-eat buffet. Mark ached to tell him to take a taste. Excitement surged through Mark, warming his skin. He sucked in a mouthful of air. The exhale rushed out of him with more laughter. "Yeah, I work here. Have since before you first came in."

He had seen the young man around enough to know his name was Scott and to know that Scott had been in the library every day. He always went for the new-releases shelf first, stacking books on the floor in front of him until the pile rose past his kneecaps, reading topics ranging from global warming to medieval weaponry and every subject in between. Scott read as much fiction too.

Mark adored intelligent men, found them sexy and passionate and focused. He also loved men who weren't afraid of him getting a little rough in bed, tying them down, controlling them.

Scott was a smart man. Did he fit the rest of the qualities Mark liked? Most guys didn't.

He sure the hell wanted to take Scott to bed and find out. No one had ever made him lose focus the way Scott did, made the desire turn to desperation so damn fast. Scott was adorable. Inquisitive. Sexy. Mark had found himself hard, his dick in his hand, in the men's room more than once after watching Scott browse the bookshelves.

If he'd only gotten one look of interest over the last four years, he would've approached Scott sooner. He wasn't into making a move when the other man didn't seem interested. He couldn't believe he hadn't taken a chance on Scott.

Better late than never.

There was interest there. Not in a "let's go on a date and see if we like each other" way so many of the men he'd propositioned over the years had looked at him. No, this was more the "please take me upstairs to the photocopy room, lay me out on the large book scanner, and fuck me stupid" way. He could go for the latter. Soon. He ached, and the other man's head was right at his crotch. What he'd give to grab a hold of Scott's hair while he fucked his mouth.

Scott had to notice Mark's lust. It wasn't like the size of his dick was hard to hide, not in its current state. Damn man was noticing too, staring at the bulge of Mark's cock, licking his lips.

Time to see if Scott was up for spending the afternoon at the library doing something other than reading.

He sat next to him. "I'm Mark."

"Hi." Scott swallowed and licked those pouty lips again. "Scott."

"Sorry if that guy was an ass to you."

Scott shrugged. "You didn't have to kick him out. It's not worth it."

"I'm surprised he hasn't given you trouble before. You're here a lot."

Scott cocked his head to the side. He was killing Mark with those big, curious eyes. Mark longed to have those eyes focused on him while he tied Scott to his bed.

"How long have you worked here?" Scott asked.

Tying him to the bed would have to wait. Mark's apartment was too far away. First, he'd get Scott alone. "Four years. I'm working on my PhD in Information Technology."

"Wow. That's neat." There was that cute-as-sin head tilt again, and those big eyes watching him. "How come I've never seen you before?"

"Guess you've always got your head in a book."

"Oh. Yeah, I guess I do." Scott dipped his head. His cheeks blazed. "What are you writing your dissertation on?"

"It looks at the modern decline of information asymmetry."

"Like people using the Internet as a way of signaling and screening?"

Yeah, this was *his* man. Mark *had* to have him. No one ever knew what the hell he was talking about. He hadn't come across anyone in a long time who he could talk to. Not anyone who could handle him in bed—handle how rough he could be, how controlling. There was just something about Scott. He would like it. He'd beg for it.

A plan formed. Mark grinned. "You like comics, huh?"

Scott lifted the comic book and stared at it like he'd forgotten it existed. "I like to read. Anything. Everything. I mean—"

Mark held up a hand. "Don't hurt yourself. I like how much you read. I work in a library, yeah? I might not read as much as you, but I do read. You're a smart man, Scott. That doesn't bother me, or scare me, or make me want you any less."

Scott bolted upright. "Really?"

"Really."

His eyes widened. "Wait. You want me? Like...*want me?*" His voice grew husky on the last of his words.

"I do. Why don't we take a ride in the elevator? The seventh-floor popular culture library has a huge collection of old comics you might like to see. You need a staff escort to enter the archives. I'd like to take you." And there were private reading cubicles with doors and real walls, instead of the flimsy partition walls most other study cubicles in the library had. No need to mention that last bit to Scott. Mark would play this out one step at a time.

Scott's tongue darted out to lick across his bottom lip. He nodded.

Mark chuckled and stood. "I'm off work in ten minutes. Meet me at the elevators." He forced himself to step away from the table and the man whose head was still bobbing in agreement. He'd clock out and head to his locker. There were condoms and lube in his bag, in case the visit to the pop culture library went as he planned.

And if it didn't?

Not possible. Scott was ready for what Mark wanted. He was sure of it.

First things first. He'd show Scott a few comic books and then show him reading wasn't the only great experience to be had at the university library.

SCOTT CLUTCHED THE comic in his hand as the dark-haired man walked away.

Mark.

Now he had a name to go with his jerk-off sessions. Although maybe there was a chance he wouldn't need to use his imagination to enjoy the man.

Mark was smart and strong and wanted him—*him*.

Scott stuffed the comic into his bag and headed for the elevators. No sense waiting any longer. If he sat too long, he might lose his nerve.

Even if Mark didn't want anything physical with him, Scott would get to see the comic archive. He hadn't ever bothered to ask if he could view the collection. That Mark had thought to show it to him was another reason in a growing list why he was rushing across the library sporting a stiff prick.

If only he could head back to his apartment and get in a little private hand time. Mark couldn't actually want to do anything with him. Not in the library. That would be…way too cool to be real. Sex in the library? With a man who looked like Mark? Reliving a moment like that would get him through the next year.

Scott quickened his pace. Hell, it'd be enough to get him through grad school.

Mark met him at the elevators ten minutes later. Scott clutched his backpack in front of his crotch, hoping it helped to hide his erection from the world but disappointed it would hide it from Mark, hide how crazy with desire he was. Surprising. He was never so bold.

Mark stepped close, ignoring the safe distance most gay guys kept to out in public. "You ready?"

The smell of Mark overwhelmed Scott again. The aroma could be bottled and sold as an aphrodisiac; it was heady and erotic and damn irresistible. Unable to stop himself, Scott leaned in. "Ready."

"Come on, then." Mark grabbed his arm, tugged him into the elevator, and hit the seventh-floor button before anyone else could slip in with them.

The hand on Scott's arm wasn't a painful grip, but it was strong and restraining, Mark's palm hot even through the shirtsleeve. The grip suggested a power Scott longed to know. He wanted to grab Mark's hand and shove it down his pants. He was *never* that bold. He loved what Mark did to him, loved how desperate and ravenous he grew just being close to him.

Once the doors closed, Mark faced him, pressing close. The force of his weight crowded Scott against the carpeted elevator wall. Mark seized Scott's waist. "I'm going to kiss you."

"Please."

Mark groaned. "I like a man who knows how to beg."

Scott could beg. It was one of the reasons most guys didn't like him. They said it made him sound needy and clingy and inexperienced. But Mark liked it. "Please kiss me."

Mark plastered his entire body against Scott. The pressure of groin against groin, chest to chest, almost had Scott rocking and going off like a kid getting his first handjob. He clutched at Mark's arms, breathing deep, hoping like hell he could keep from shooting in his pants once their lips met.

Mark paused. Their mouths so close, his breath heated Scott's lips. He said, "You have the best mouth. I want to taste those lips."

Scott whimpered. He couldn't stop it from spilling out. It was as uncontrolled as breathing.

"I like that sound, Scott." Mark leaned forward and brought their mouths together, a brush of warm lips. He slid his tongue across Scott's lower lip, tasting, teasing. The kiss was soft and slow and not like any Scott had ever known. It consumed him. He wanted more of Mark, needed more of his tongue, his lips, his hands. He twisted his fingers in Mark's shirtsleeves and tugged.

Mark shoved his body against Scott and smashed their mouths

together, turning the kiss urgent. His hands landed on Scott's ass, and he dug in, grinding their groins together.

The pull of that grip, the sharp jab of the nails as they buried in his ass, had Scott's balls drawing up. He was close. He whimpered again, the sound muffling as it filled Mark's mouth.

A chime sounded above their heads.

Mark jerked away, keeping the grip of his right hand on Scott's ass for a moment more. When the doors slid open, Mark removed his hand and strode out of the elevator.

His breath hitching, Scott leaned against the wall. He closed his eyes and focused on getting air into his lungs.

As the fog in his mind cleared, he opened his eyes. Mark smiled at him from where he stood outside the elevator next to a set of glass doors.

Scott pushed away from the wall, hoping like hell he could keep from tripping. He had to get back to touching Mark, had to know what else Mark could do to him, what else the man could give him. Like a needle in a compass, pointing to true north, he made his way to him in no time.

WHAT THE HELL had happened between the first floor and the seventh?

The idea of fooling around in a private library cubicle had Mark hot and bothered, sure. Making out like a couple of teenagers, groping in the damn elevator where anyone could have seen them when the doors opened? That was crazy and risky and salacious as fuck.

The way Scott had looked at him, clutched, rocked, his body begging for more, had Mark losing all his resolve. He'd meant to take a quick taste. See if Scott would resist a simple kiss so he'd know which way the wind was blowing. He didn't mean for it to go from zero to ninety so fast. He simply couldn't stop it. The way Scott trembled under his touch as the kiss intensified almost had him turning him around, ripping off their pants, and fucking him right there in the elevator. Screw his job.

Mark liked his sex intense, but he'd never been with someone who responded with such immediate need. Scott's hunger called to him.

As Scott moved from the elevator to his side, those wide eyes watched Mark, never looking away. It was invigorating—how much the younger man wanted him. It gave him all sorts of ideas on how to torment Scott, tease him until he begged to come.

Forget the comics-of-yesteryears tour. He'd be seeing Scott again. He'd have to. There'd be time for dating and dinner and tours of the library later. Then a thought occurred to him. A creative, wonderful, tantalizing thought. Mark headed for the glass doors.

"Wait," Scott said, his voice breathless, shaky. He shifted on his feet. "I was thinking…if you want to, we could go somewhere else…instead."

Mark smiled again and went to Scott. He ran a hand through the blond hair and followed the curve of his cheek to those kiss-swollen, wet lips. "Trust me. I won't keep you waiting. Not for long." He pushed through the doors and showed his ID at the archive desk, taking note of the few people and employees browsing the stacks. If they only knew what he and Scott were about to do not thirty feet away. He faced Scott.

The other man stood inside the doors. Those curious eyes were huge again, taking it all in. Books, CDs, cassettes, magazines, dime novels, fanzines, postcards, and other published works filled the shelves and racks of the extensive popular culture collection. Framed trading cards covered the walls. Giant movie posters from films like *Casablanca*, *From Here to Eternity*, and Hitchcock's *The Birds* hung from ceiling cables in a gallery-style display.

Mark's gut churned. Was this one of his worst ideas ever? Now that Scott saw the collection, he might not look at him again. At least not like he had before.

Time to put his plan in motion.

He advanced. He leaned close to Scott and whispered in his ear, letting his lips and breath brush over skin. "You can look at whatever you'd like, but the comic collection is this way." He gestured toward a long hall that led to a back room.

Scott stared at him. That delectable "take me" look was back. Mark stepped away and released a sigh as Scott followed.

Inside the comics room, they were alone again. Mark closed the door. "Browse around. I've got something in particular to show you." He punched in a quick search at the catalog station. It didn't take long to locate the issue. He tucked it under his arm.

Scott wandered from shelf to shelf, pulling out one binder of old comics after another. The lithe body and curious eyes were driving Mark crazy. He wanted to touch Scott again. Either that or he had to get himself the hell home. He palmed his own erection and gave himself a few good rubs through his pants before pulling away. It was time for Scott to give him what he needed—what they both needed.

"Scott."

He poked his head around the corner of a bookshelf. "Huh?"

"Come here," Mark said, his voice stern, commanding.

Scott came to him. His lower lip quivered as they stared at each other. Mark brushed his thumb over the shaking lip. Scott's tongue snaked out, and he sucked Mark's finger into the wet heat of his mouth. Such a beautiful mouth.

"I've got something to show you. Have a seat."

Scott released his thumb and pouted.

Mark almost pulled him into his arms and forced their mouths together again. No. The private study room before they went further. If they kissed, he wouldn't be able to stop again. The next time Scott was in his arms, they were getting a hell of a lot more naked.

Scott reached for the chair at a nearby table.

"Not there." Mark pointed to the door of the closest study room. "In there."

Scott darted for the room.

It was lovely—the way he followed his commands, the way Scott sought to please him.

Mark's expectations were high.

He smiled. Scott would not disappoint.

IT WAS ALL so unbelievable. Scott was in one of his favorite places, surrounded by books—comic books, no less, the type he'd enjoyed since first learning to read—heading to a private study room, followed by a gorgeous, assertive man. Whatever Mark was about to show him, give to him, Scott was desperate for it.

His body craved it.

He stepped into the study room. It was small, with two simple wood chairs and a long table covered in scratches and pen marks, names and numbers scrawled amid the amateur artwork. If he wanted a good time, there was a girl named Carly who seemed promising. And popular. Lucky for him, he wanted something else. He dropped his backpack to a chair, willing the shake in his hands to stop. The thud of his heartbeat echoed in his ears.

The door closed behind him.

"Sit," Mark said.

Scott sat. It seemed the minute Mark asked something of him, his body obliged. Nothing had ever seemed so simple, so right, so visceral.

Mark pressed close behind him, rubbing his groin against Scott's neck.

Scott whimpered and closed his eyes. He turned his head to the side. Mark shifted, brushing the bulge of his erection against Scott's cheek.

It was instinct, a driving force that spurred Scott to action. His lips spread. He mouthed the evidence of Mark's arousal, wetting and sucking through the fabric. He felt empty everywhere. His ass. His mouth. He needed to expose Mark's cock. Get it into his mouth without the clothes in the way.

He loved sucking dick. The sleek skin over the hard, full shaft. The way it filled his mouth, slid over his lips, throbbed against his tongue as it hardened more, it all incited his own desire, urged him on. He lifted his hands and grasped the zipper on Mark's pants.

Mark grabbed his wrists. "Not yet. Hold on to the back legs of the chair."

Scott clutched the chair and arched his back, continuing his attention on Mark's cock. He opened his mouth wider, moving up the fabric in search of the sensitive head, desperate to give Mark the best he had to offer.

The heat of Mark's body disappeared, leaving Scott bare, alone.

Mark's breath drifted over his earlobe. "Have you seen this before?"

A comic book lay on the table in front of Scott. He gasped. The cover was…well, like no other comic he had read before. He'd seen some amateur drawings online but never anything like this on a cover. Two men on a bed, both shirtless, one on top of the other, exchanging a kiss, their bodies pressed close, chest against chest.

Mark nipped along his earlobe. Then his tongue followed the same path. "Have you never seen an erotic comic book?"

"No. They don't have these at Main Street Comics."

"I wouldn't think so. That place is rather tame. The popular culture library has several pieces containing…explicit content." Mark reached over Scott's shoulder and opened the book. He flipped pages, then stopped halfway.

Scott's cock would have moaned and begged if it could evoke sound. In one panel, a small, naked blond man was bent face-first over a table, his arms stretched over his head, his wrists tied together by a blue cloth. The end of a long glove. A tall, brawny man wearing only a mask and cape was kneeling behind the blond and had his tongue between the man's ass cheeks. In another panel, the tall masked man was pressed on top of the blond with his cock buried in the smaller man. The blond man's face was contorted in an explosive moment of bliss.

It had been a while since Scott was with anyone other than his own hand, but even when he was with a man, he'd never expressed his orgasm like the man in the picture.

He released his grip on the chair. Would touching the image help him understand that look?

Mark's firm hand seized his wrist, stilling him. Mark knelt beside Scott and wound a strip of cloth around his arm and tied a knot. The restraint mashed against the inside of Scott's wrist. A black tie with a splash of red. Mark tugged on the tie, forcing Scott's arm against the chair leg but not tying him to it.

Mark's tie restraining him only had Scott longing for the tie around his other arm, over his eyes, for Mark to tie him down and fuck him into oblivion.

"This picture," Mark said. "It's what I want to do to you. Right now."

Scott buried his face in Mark's neck. He inhaled the crisp scent and said the only word that made its way through his muddled brain. "Please."

MARK SNAPPED HIS hips forward. Scott's begging had him undone. His control shattered, he snaked a hand around Scott's neck and captured his mouth in a kiss. He had planned on demanding Scott give him a blowjob with that incredible mouth, but he needed in him. Now.

He had to calm down, regain control before they went any further, or he'd never make it until he got them undressed.

The kiss was doing nothing to abate his raging craze to be with this man. Scott's tongue tangled with his, pushing, then going shallow again, finally letting Mark lead the chase.

Mark pulled back. He had to rein in his lust, take control of the moment for both of them. Give them more than kissing and coming in their own pants. Give them what they both craved.

Scott's gaze met his. "Why do you want me?"

Did he not know his own appeal? Didn't he understand the draw he had? The power?

"You are sexy as hell. I've wanted you for a long time." Mark yanked on the tie. Scott's arm lifted, and he stood. "And it's time to show you how much I want you." Mark released his grasp on the tie, attacked Scott's T-shirt, and hauled it over his head. The exposed skin offered too good a diversion. He ducked his head and tongued a hard nipple.

Scott threaded a hand through Mark's hair, clutching and releasing over and over, moaning and rocking his pelvis.

Mark continued his assault, twirling his tongue around the sensitive nub, scraping it with his teeth, then pinching and tugging. He worked Scott's pants open, dying to reach more skin, to touch his cock. Once the pants were past Scott's hips, Mark released him. "Step out of your shoes and pants."

Scott did as he was told.

Mark grabbed Scott's shoulders and turned him. He held him tight, back to chest, and stepped forward until Scott's thighs struck the edge of the table. He shoved him to lie face-first across the table and said, "Put your hands above your head."

Mark reached for the black silk tie dangling from one of Scott's wrists. He wound the fabric around the other wrist and secured it so Scott's hands met, palms together. There was nothing like the moment when he was still dressed and a naked, willing, submissive man was spread out bare before him. The power, the thrill, the commanding vision got to him. If he hadn't been so desperate to fuck Scott, he'd extend the moment, make Scott writhe and beg. But the time for such delights had passed.

Scott shifted, rocking his ass backward. "Please."

Mark shouldn't have doubted him. Scott had already been more of what he longed for in a lover than anyone else. Ever.

Mark reached a shaking hand to his pants, unzipped them, and released his own cock. It sprang free as if it could seek out Scott's body on its own, get inside him without any assistance from his brain.

Scott rocked again and groaned. Was he searching out a connection with Mark's body? Or was he looking for friction for his own dick? It didn't matter; Scott was right where Mark wanted him. Incoherent. Lost. Drowning.

And it was time for him to help.

He swept a hand along Scott's spine and over his ass. He gripped his thighs. "Don't move. And try to be quiet. We don't want to be interrupted."

"No," Scott cried out. His next words were muffled as he bit his lip. "I need you."

Mark dropped to his knees. He spread Scott's ass open wide and leaned in, tracing a long path with his tongue.

Scott whimpered.

The sound spurred Mark on. He returned to the bit of flesh surrounding the entrance to Scott's body. He traced around it with the tip of his tongue, loving the way Scott shook and twitched from that one touch connecting them. He pressed his tongue flat, giving the other man as many sensations as he could, and then he pushed his tongue in.

Scott groaned and rocked into his touch. His reactions were so sensual, so needy.

Mark grasped Scott's ass in his hands. If he didn't, he'd grip his own cock and stroke himself to orgasm. There was no way in hell he was getting off until he was inside Scott.

He stood and ditched his own clothes, grabbing a condom and the lube before kicking his pants aside. "Going to make you feel good. Going to fuck you so hard, you'll never come into the library again without getting a hard-on. You'll never read a comic again without coming in your pants." Mark would've stood there stroking himself while he spoke to Scott, telling him what he planned to do to him—it was how he always liked to begin—but three pulls and he'd shoot all over Scott's back. So he sheathed his dick and slicked it up. He added more lube to his fingers and worked them inside the other man, loving the way Scott moaned and thrashed beneath him.

"Are you ready for me?" Mark asked. "God, can't wait."

"Yes!" Scott lifted his head. "Are you... Did you..."

Mark rubbed Scott's back. "Got the rubber on. Don't worry. I'll take care of you. In more ways than one."

Scott exhaled and dropped his forehead to the table again.

Mark brought his dick to Scott's body, took a deep breath, and slid in, grunting as the muscles of Scott's ass gripped him. He sucked in a sharp breath, fighting the urge to plunge in and out.

Then the fight was over. He couldn't hold still. Scott was begging and rocking again. Mark pulled back and shoved in, beginning a fierce pace, slamming his hips against Scott's ass.

"Will you," Scott said. "Will you...oh..."

Mark forced his body to stop and placed a hand on Scott's lower back. "What? What do you need?"

"Will you...my ass? Hit me? Hold me down?" Scott's body vibrated as the words left his mouth. His restrained arms shook.

"My God, yes." Mark pinned Scott to the table, raised his other hand, and smacked Scott's ass. The slap, the slight rise of color, there was nothing else like it. The rush. Pushing someone to the edge. He raised his hand again. When his palm made contact, Scott moaned and trembled. Mark pressed down on Scott's back harder. "Don't come. Not yet."

"Oh, please. Please, Mark."

He smacked Scott's ass again. "No." Mark quickened his pace, driving into Scott faster, harder. Scott's begging, the shudders of his body, the way he met Mark with each thrust, all had Mark unraveling. He held out for as long as he could. It wasn't long. He reached around and stroked Scott's dick. "Now."

Scott came, his ass seizing Mark's cock.

Mark gripped at Scott's hips as he pulled the man back onto him, grasping the flesh in each hand as his orgasm crashed over him. Every shudder racked his body. When he finally stilled, he collapsed against Scott's back.

Faint voices in the room outside registered, but absolutely nothing mattered.

He'd just had the best damn orgasm of his life.

SCOTT DRIFTED IN the haze of climax. Words floated through his head, but none fit where he'd been. He sighed. "Wow."

Mark rolled off and onto the table next to him. "You liked that?"

Scott tried to lift his head. It wouldn't move. It'd be a while before he'd be able to stand, let alone walk. "Uh-huh. Couldn't you tell?" He was never going to forget. He'd have trouble making it home before he wanted to jerk off to memories of what they'd done. No one had ever talked to him like that, pushed him, taken control when he needed him to.

Mark untied his wrists, rubbed the flesh with an open palm. He helped Scott roll over onto his back. "Yeah," Mark said. "It was like nothing else."

Oh. The experience had been powerful, intense. And not just for Scott. For Mark too.

Mark leaned over him and asked, "What are you doing tomorrow morning?"

"Uh…reading?"

Mark shook his head.

"Studying?"

Mark gave another shake.

"Sleeping in your bed?" Did he say that out loud?

"That's right. You're coming home with me tonight—where I have a bed."

"Okay."

"And handcuffs."

"Oh."

"And where we can be loud."

Scott smiled. Mark was going to give him so much of what he craved. "That would be…better than any book."

Chapter Two

"Damn. Scott Murphy in my apartment." Mark couldn't believe it. He folded his arms across his chest, leaned against the closed door, and watched the man he'd just fucked on the seventh-floor of the university library walk into his living room.

Scott spun around to face him. "You know my last name?"

"Sure I do."

Even from across the room Mark could see Scott's face flush before he gripped the strap on the backpack slung over his shoulder and turned away.

This was going to be even more enjoyable than Mark had imagined earlier when he'd been lying naked across the table in the library study room, a sweaty, spent Scott beside him.

Scott moved farther into the small living room, his steps light and quiet, as if he thought they were still in the library. He had a disheveled look about him as he clutched his backpack tighter. Did he always protect that bag with his life? Or maybe he was nervous. Which was endearing after what they'd done in that study room. His hair was stuck up in the front where his forehead had been pressing against the table earlier. A reminder of their time together.

Mark liked that.

"What's your last name?" Scott asked, his voice low. Maybe he was afraid he was dreaming and if he spoke any louder he'd end the moment.

If this was a dream, Mark had no intention of waking until he'd had another go with Scott, until he had a chance to touch him everywhere, really explore his body like he hadn't done yet. He laughed, less at his own thoughts than the idea that Scott had never noticed him or been aware of who he was, while Mark had been watching Scott for years. "Lewis," he said.

"Mark Lewis." Scott mouthed the name twice more without a sound, like he was trying it out or hoping he'd remember it after he left. The latter sounded good. Mark wanted Scott to have all sorts of reasons to remember him.

Four years he'd spent picturing Scott in his apartment—in his bed. Why the hell had he thought the man wasn't interested? One look at Scott in the library earlier, sitting there clutching his backpack and the *Red Arch-rival* comic book, his eyes wide as he looked up at him, and Mark knew Scott would want what he'd always imagined doing to him, what they'd done in that study room. And more.

"Are you sure this is okay?" Scott asked.

"Is what okay?"

"That I'm here." He stared at his sneakers and bit his bottom lip. "It's getting late."

"It is. Which is why I asked you here. I wanted to spend more time together, and the library was closing." He wanted Scott to be all his for the entire night. He had so many ideas, so many ways he wanted to play. Ways he wanted to pleasure Scott, push him to the edge.

He couldn't believe how relaxed he was about it. Usually he second-guessed himself, second-guessed that any man he was with would want to go as far as he did. Most guys didn't like being tied up. Or teased. They wanted to get off. Fast and often. They weren't up for the long sessions where he liked to take control, to draw out the pleasure, to hear a man begging for him.

Scott would love all of it. Just like he did when he'd begged Mark to hold him down on that table in the study room, to spank him across the ass.

No other sexual moment of Mark's life had been as intense—or as pleasurable. No one had ever matched his desires the way Scott had.

He wasn't ready to give that up. Not yet.

Two weeks until his dissertation defense. Graduation three and a half months after that, then he'd be moving from Ohio to Seattle, Washington where he'd already had three phone interviews with community colleges. Until then, there was time. Hell, even one night with Scott would be better than nothing.

If Bruce Kreger hadn't been such a jackass at the library, then Scott might never have looked at Mark, and Mark might never have made a move to get them in that study room. Guess he owed the jackass a thank-you.

A near miss.

What little time they'd have together wasn't getting away from him now. He had to know what Scott would look like tied to his bed.

Scott wandered around the living room, examining the space like he thought he'd be quizzed on it later. The apartment wasn't spacious by any stretch of the imagination, but there was a lot to see where a man like Scott was concerned. Five bookcases covered the walls, each filled from top to bottom. Mysteries, thrillers, classics, textbooks, and how-to guides. Random spaces between the books held the trophies and medals Mark had treasured for years. The walls on either side of the bookshelves displayed even more awards.

He smirked as Scott stopped before the largest bookcase and reached for a leather-bound book. His hand stilled before he touched the spine, and he swung to face Mark. "You live alone?"

"I do. I spent all of undergrad living in a house with seven other guys and almost the same thing during my master's program. I wanted my own space this time around." He pushed away from the door and made his way to Scott. "It isn't much. One bedroom and the bathroom, not even a real kitchen." A sink, microwave, compact fridge, and single-burner hot plate lined one wall on the other side of the carpeted living space. Other than the bookshelves, there was a red and orange plaid couch that had come with the apartment and was probably as old as he, and a huge computer desk that held his laptop and three desktop computers he was in the process of repairing for friends and coworkers. The desk was also covered in open books and journals, legal pads of paper, and printed articles marked with highlighted passages. It was the only space where he wasn't a neat freak. Over the past four years his dissertation had consumed his life.

"It's fantastic." Scott sounded in awe. He hiked his backpack higher on his shoulder and licked his lips as he glanced at Mark. "I'd love to have my own place like this." He turned back to the bookshelf, cocked his head to the side, and browsed the collection without touching a single book.

Mark wanted to run his hand through the blond hair. Wanted to taste Scott's pouty lips again. But he also wanted to talk with Scott, get to know him. Not something he'd ever felt with the guys he'd been with since his last steady boyfriend five years ago.

"You'll have your own place someday. You're paying your dues, going to school." He stepped behind Scott and leaned in. He couldn't help himself. He ran his lips along the side of Scott's neck. He could smell the result of their activities earlier in the library, the scent of sweat and sex. All male. Exhilarating. Intoxicating. He slid his hand up Scott's arm and lifted the backpack off his shoulder, then lowered the bag to the floor.

Scott's hand clenched like he didn't want to let the bag go, but he did.

"Anything on that bookcase you haven't read?" Mark asked.

"Uh…"

Mark ducked his head again and swiped his tongue along the flesh of Scott's neck. Scott gasped, and he shivered. The reaction was delicious. Another step closer, and Mark pressed against his back. He paused for a moment to let Scott feel the weight of his body against him; then he whispered, "Tell me."

"I've read all these."

Not unexpected, but still impressive. "Even this one?" Mark reached over Scott's shoulder and pointed to a book from his Evaluation of Artificial Intelligence class. Even he hadn't read it cover to cover. Five hundred pages of dry in-depth history of the theory and programming languages of AI.

"Yeah," Scott said. "I saw it at the university bookstore."

"So you bought a copy even though you weren't taking the class?"

Scott shook his head. "I didn't buy it. I sat on the floor and read it. They like me there so they don't give me a hard time about stuff like that." He shrugged, rubbing Mark's shirt over his nipples with the movement.

Mark squeezed his eyes shut for a moment, then opened them and forced himself to concentrate on the conversation. "You read the entire book in one sitting?"

"No. I got halfway through and then the bookstore closed. I had to go back after class the next day to finish it."

And people said Mark read like a fanatic. He was an amateur next to Scott. Mark lifted a hand and rubbed the length of Scott's arm again, this time snaking his hand under the cuff of the T-shirt, lingering over the flesh of Scott's biceps. "What's your favorite book?"

"Ever?" Scott asked.

"Ever."

"That's…an impossible question." He raised his hand to the bookshelf again, getting an inch from the same book as before, then dropped his hand to his own thigh and gripped the seam of his pants instead.

"Go ahead. You can touch anything you want." He'd meant the books, but he could go for Scott's hands on his body. And soon.

"Thanks." Scott pulled the book he'd been after off the shelf. *Of Mice and Men*. He flipped through it, stopping at the pages Mark had dog-eared.

Mark swiped his fingers over the ones Scott had curled around the edge of the book, and explored Scott's neck on the opposite side with his mouth. So damn responsive, Scott leaned into the touch of both hand and lips.

"You can't pick a favorite?" Mark pressed his cock to the top of Scott's ass and spoke the words without removing his lips from Scott's soft, musky-scented skin.

Scott breathed deep a few times, baring his neck more before he answered. "I guess it'd be the first book I fell in love with as a kid." His voice hitched as Mark slid his tongue into the touch.

Mark began a slow shift of his hips, rubbing his hardening cock against the top of Scott's ass, just enough so they both could feel it. He wanted more, wanted Scott to drop the book and grab him instead. He'd wait a little longer. "Which book was that?" he asked.

"*My Side of the Mountain.*" Scott slowly closed *Of Mice and Men*, letting their hands keep contact for a moment longer before returning the book to the shelf. With his other arm, and without turning to face Mark, he slid his hand around the back of Mark's neck, like he'd been reading his mind and knew how much he'd been craving that contact. The touch of Scott's tentative fingers was electric. Then his hand shook.

Nerves? Or something more?

Scott spoke again, his voice as shaky as his touch. "I never went outside much as a kid. I was always in my room. Studying. Reading. Hiding. After I read that book, I felt like I'd done it, like I'd run away and lived off the land. Reading lets you do all kinds of things. Lets you go anywhere. Do anything."

"Did you want to run away when you were a kid?"

"No. I could never leave my dad. I just thought it sounded brave."

Mark moved his hips faster, loving Scott sharing something personal. Scott gripped the back of Mark's neck and groaned, his hips moving in time with Mark's now.

"Like that comic book today?" Mark asked. He traveled his palm up Scott's arm again, massaging as he went. "Did you feel like you'd had your ass licked, like you'd been fucked over a table when you'd seen those pictures?"

"No." Scott tilted his head backward, almost resting it on Mark's shoulder. "Seeing it was nothing like when you did it to me."

Mark didn't usually fish for compliments, but he relished hearing the words from Scott, the confirmation that it had been intense for him too.

Without warning, Scott dropped his arm and stepped to the side. He ran a shaking hand through his hair, giving it an even more disheveled look.

"Something wrong?"

"No." Scott swept the tips of his fingers over a shelf of books as he walked away from Mark. "You have a lot of books."

Mark wanted to follow, but he held still. "I bet you do too."

"Not really. I can't afford it. I always have the maximum checked out from the library, though." He stopped before a tall, thin bookcase. Mark's favorites. Scott stood on his toes and pulled a book from the top shelf. *Love and Conquer in the Time of War*. He scanned the dust jacket.

"You read that one too?"

Scott nodded. "I liked it. I like most historical fiction. My major's history." He set the edge of the book on the shelf and used one finger to slide it in place, his touch gentle, as if it were an original copy of a Shakespeare play. When he faced Mark, Scott had his lower lip pinched between his teeth again. Their gazes locked, and Scott let out a long breath, that lip quivering as he released it. "I liked it a lot."

"That book?"

Scott shook his head. "Today. What you did to me."

Mark took a step forward. "Me too."

They stared for several breaths; then Scott whirled to face the bookshelf again.

Mark couldn't keep away. He crossed the room and pinned Scott against the shelf. "I liked what you did to me too."

"What *I* did? I hardly did anything."

"Believe me, you did a lot."

A tremble moved through Scott's body.

"Are you scared of me?" Mark had to ask, had to be sure.

"No."

"Excited?"

"Yes."

"Good. I'd like to talk some more, but I can't seem to keep from touching you. You're gorgeous. And irresistible."

"So are you. Can I…"

"What?"

"Can I touch you again?"

"Hell yes. Touch me wherever you'd like."

Scott reached backward and brushed a hand over Mark's ass.

Damn pants. Mark wanted to feel the touch of skin on skin again. He worked his own hand under the front of Scott's T-shirt and grazed one nipple with his thumb. Scott whimpered and clutched at Mark's ass. "Please."

God, that beg sounded even better than at the library. "Please what?"

"Something. Anything. Touch me. Fuck me."

Mark raised Scott's shirt higher and drew it over his head, disappointed when Scott had to let go of his ass but not enough to stop where they were headed. He kissed the skin between Scott's shoulder blades and ran his palm down his back, loving the slight shudder of Scott's body as he glided hand and mouth lower.

He settled on his knees behind Scott. "Undo your pants."

Without delay, he heard the slide of the zipper, and Mark lowered the pants, purposely taking Scott's underwear with them. As he exposed each inch of flesh, he kissed and licked the skin. First one ass cheek, then the other. Working lower and lower, he nipped and sucked on the warm flesh, leaving small red marks in his wake, Scott whimpering and shifting with each touch of tongue and teeth on his skin.

Mark slid Scott's shoes and socks off, then the underwear and pants. He stood and placed a chaste kiss at the back of Scott's neck. "Wait here for me."

Scott turned his head. He was breathing hard, his mouth open, his lips wet like he'd been licking or sucking on them. "Where are you going?"

"I'll be right back." Mark cupped the back of Scott's head and forced him to face the books. He raised Scott's arms above him and wrapped his fingers around each end of the bookcase so his arms formed a V above his head. "I'm not leaving you. Don't move. Wait right like this."

Scott made a small sound—part whimper, part affirmation.

Nice. Mark smirked as he stepped away and entered his bedroom. He opened the top drawer of his dresser. Bondage tape? Not yet. Handcuffs? Wouldn't work with the shelves. Rope? Yes. The thin red rope. It would look lovely against Scott's skin. Scott would be able to see it wound around the bookcase and his wrists. He wouldn't be able to deny he was tied up.

The breath caught in Mark's chest as he walked into the living room. Scott hadn't moved. He still held on to the bookcase, his forehead resting against the row of books before him, his heavy, uneven exhales visible with each breath.

Damn sexy man. Doing exactly as he'd been told.

Without touching any other part of him, Mark secured the rope around Scott's right wrist. Scott lifted his head at the contact and watched as Mark wrapped the rope around his arm.

"This rope is new. I've never used it on anyone."

Scott made another desperate sound. It turned into a low moan, and his hips moved, pushing his ass back to meet Mark's groin.

"Patience," Mark said, but he could hear the anticipation in his own tone. Scott was probably too far gone into the sensations to notice. "The bookcase is anchored to the wall, so don't worry about it falling on us." He worked the rope behind the bookcase twice and bound Scott's other arm. He gripped Scott's head and forced him to look to the side, then without warning planted a long, deep kiss on his lips. The sweet, slow slide of Scott's tongue against his own was better than any kiss they'd exchanged yet. Scott made another sound. Something about that slight, frustrated whimper and the way he pulled on the ropes was a little too familiar.

A little too much like the last time with Dale. Mark stepped back. "Do you want me to stop?"

Scott looked over his shoulder with wide eyes. "What?"

"The rope. We don't have to because—"

"I want to!" Scott gripped an edge of the bookcase in each hand. "I like it. No one…no one usually wants to."

"That's what I thought." He moved in close behind Scott again, their bodies touching along their lengths. "Just needed to hear you say it." He rubbed his erection along Scott's ass, loving the look of his clothed body and Scott's bare skin coming together.

Scott threw his head back to Mark's shoulder. "Oh God, please."

He laughed. "It's not necessary to call me God, but I do like the sound of it." That brought out a laugh from Scott too. He lifted his head, and Mark tucked a few strands of blond hair behind Scott's ear, then followed it with a swipe of his tongue along his earlobe. He whispered, "I want to hear you call out my name. I want to hear you scream for me."

"Yes, Mark! I want that too."

That deserved a reward. Mark worked his tie open—the same black tie with the splash of red he'd used on Scott earlier—and held it up beside them.

It was clear the moment Scott saw the tie. He sucked in a quick breath.

"Do you like being blindfolded?" Mark asked.

"I…I think so."

"Close your eyes."

Scott held still as Mark positioned the tie and secured it over his eyes.

"You tell me if you want this off or if you need me to untie you for any reason."

Scott nodded.

That wasn't good enough. "I need you to say it. You'll tell me to stop if you need me to."

"I will. I promise."

"Good." Mark threw his dress shirt off, wrestled his pants open, and slid them down his legs. Dammit. The lube and condom were in his pocket. He hiked up his pants again, got out the necessary items, and kicked the clothes aside. He was never this out of control.

He forced the words out as slow and even as he could manage. "Spread your legs."

Scott did as he was told. Mark got the condom on and used the lube on himself, then Scott. Too much lube, but he had every intention of ramming into Scott hard and fast as many times as he could before he exploded. He wasn't taking any chances he'd actually cause Scott serious pain. That wasn't his thing.

Scott didn't hold still as Mark touched his asshole with the lubed fingers. He wiggled and writhed, bucking back and forth as Mark's finger hit his gland. His dick had to be rubbing all over the books. That thought did nothing to help Mark fend off the desperate need to come.

He could smell Scott's desire combined with the aroma of the books all around them. His small living room always smelled like a used bookstore whenever he stepped inside the apartment, but being so close to the shelves, the scent of paper and glue and a bit of dust was stronger. His mom had given him a number of first editions over the years. He held back a laugh at the thought that they might end up ruining one or two of them.

It didn't matter. He loved books, but they were nothing compared to the real flesh-and-blood man standing before him. A man Mark longed to know, to spend more than one night with.

Four months until he graduated, until he headed across the country. Four months would never be enough. He forced the thought away. It didn't matter right then.

He had to fuck Scott again. This time against the books, let Scott breathe in their scent, let him feel the leather and paper spines rub against his cock.

He grabbed Scott by the hip, spread his own legs to find the right height, brought his dick to Scott's ass, and surged forward until the head of his cock made its way inside. Scott's knuckles turned white where he gripped the bookshelf. He dropped his head and smacked his forehead on the row of books before him.

Mark reached around and rubbed Scott's forehead, then moved his hand lower and gripped one of Scott's nipples between two fingers.

He tugged in time with his thrusts as he worked his way inside Scott's body.

Scott arched on his toes and stuck his ass out farther, the ropes pulling taut as his body bent. The bright red rope against Scott's skin looked amazing. Mark wanted to see it wrapped around Scott's every limb, his thighs, his chest, his groin, his cock and balls. Would Scott like such intense bondage?

Later. He'd find out later.

He let go of all thoughts and concerns. With each thrust, he buried deep into Scott and reveled in the moans that poured out of the other man, the way Scott's ass clenched around him. He was close already. They both were. Mark had barely had a chance to drag out the pleasure, to tease Scott. He'd never been so lost, so far from the control he longed for. Which just confirmed that he'd have to have more of Scott Murphy.

He ran his hand lower and lower until he gripped Scott's cock. The tip was wet. Mark liked the idea of smelling Scott's release on the leather-bound books later. He moved his hand down the shaft, then fisted it to the tip in one quick grip.

"Mark!" Scott cried out, shuddering again and again. His ass clenched tighter and didn't let up.

That did it. No matter how much Mark wanted this to go on, he couldn't stop the flood of sensation and release. He came, grunting and slowing his thrusts as Scott's body pulled the orgasm out of him.

He waited a moment until he caught his breath. This part was almost better than his own orgasm. He began a quick stroke of Scott's cock. "Your turn."

Scott groaned, and Mark worked him through the spasms, loving that Scott was so uninhibited as his body jerked, as he cried out Mark's name again and again. Was he always that loud? Or was it because they were no longer in the library? Was it the ropes? The blindfold? Or was it being with Mark that drove him wild with pleasure?

Scott stilled a moment later and slumped against the books. The quiet in the wake of his screams and Mark's grunts was unnerving. Which was odd. Mark was usually fine with the quiet, with being alone in his apartment. He closed his eyes and listened to the rhythmic breathing from Scott as he came down from the rush. The unease washed away. Mark stepped back and got rid of the condom, but he wasn't ready to let go of Scott. He pressed close again, gripped Scott's wrists, and leaned against his back.

Scott sighed, sounding content, amazed, but a moment later he tensed. "I'm sorry." He pushed away from the bookshelf. "Oh, God. I shouldn't have. I'm sorry."

"It's okay." Mark undid the tie covering Scott's eyes and let it fall to the floor. He unfastened one wrist, then the other before Scott could hurt himself pushing away from the shelves with such determination. "You shouldn't have what?"

Scott lowered his arms but kept his back to Mark. "I ruined your books."

"They're just books. That was worth getting any one of them sticky." Mark turned Scott to face him. He cupped his chin, forcing him to look up. "Besides, I like having the reminder you were here."

SCOTT WAS DREAMING. He had to be.

Mark Lewis was the perfect mix of erotic strength and a gentle touch. A nice guy who knew how to give Scott everything he craved when it came to sex—things he'd only imagined before, things he'd never thought he'd ever get the chance to experience. Guys like this didn't exist. And no one had such powerful, amazing sex twice in one day. That only happened in pornos.

Oh God. Mark probably thought he was easy. Did he think Scott did this with every guy who came on to him? Did he think guys came on to him a lot? Because no one had in such a long time, it was embarrassing to admit.

In fact, nothing close to what they'd done ever happened. Not to Scott.

He realized he'd been staring into Mark's eyes, probably looking like some kind of lovesick kid. He forced himself to glance around Mark's apartment instead. For a brief moment he pictured himself curled up on the ugliest couch he'd ever seen, reading a book while Mark worked at the oversize computer desk. A perfect moment.

But the baseball and soccer trophies and awards... Mark was a sports guy.

They shared a love of books, but it didn't look like they had anything else in common.

Just sex.

This would never be more than one night. They'd never spend a lazy Sunday together reading and working. How silly of him to even picture it.

Mark was still staring at him, his gaze traveling up and down Scott's body until he paused at his groin. "Nice." He reached out and ran the tip of his index finger over the tattoo below Scott's left hip bone. A dragon. Small, barely an inch high, but colorful. No one else had ever seen it except the tattoo artist. It was hard to miss the way Mark was checking it out. Scott felt naked.

Well, he was naked, but it felt more intense than merely being physically bare. Like he'd exposed a part of himself he never let anyone see.

He wanted to get dressed, but he didn't want to come off like an embarrassed virgin. What with Mark also still naked.

That gave Scott something else to focus on. Mark was gorgeous, every ounce of his body tight and firm. His skin had a bronze glow to it like he'd spent a week vacationing somewhere tropical. Scott longed to caress his flesh again. Mark's flaccid cock was also a temptation. Scott wanted it in his mouth, wanted to lick and suck until he made Mark hard with just his mouth. But they'd already had sex. Twice. The sight before Scott was too good. He'd be hard again soon just thinking about that body pressed against his back, that beautiful dick inside his ass. How embarrassing would it be to get another stiff one so soon? He'd really look like a kid then. Like a kid who never got laid.

He forced himself to focus on something else. "Have you read all these books?"

When Mark didn't answer, Scott glanced back at him. Mark was smirking. What was so funny? Maybe he really did see Scott as an inexperienced kid.

"Almost all of them," Mark finally said. He pointed to another bookcase Scott hadn't looked at yet. "The ones there are my to-read stack."

Scott glanced over the titles. "They're all good. Especially the four on the right." He could discuss a couple of those books for hours, but he held back the instinct. He felt better focusing on Mark's selection of books, but he could easily go overboard. "You have good taste."

Mark raised his hand and slid his palm over Scott's cheek. He swiped the pad of his thumb along his jawline, then lower, down the sensitive skin of his neck. "I do."

Oh, God. Scott couldn't take this. Mark was too nice—too much of what he wanted from a boyfriend, that blend of rough control and soft caring. Scott eyed his pants and shirt, but where the hell were his underwear? He'd definitely had them on, because he would never forget the way Mark had taken them off. He gave up on the underwear and scrambled for his pants. "I should go. I have homework…" He lifted a leg to slide the pants on and spotted his underwear poking out from beneath his T-shirt.

"Don't," Mark said, his voice firm but not loud or mean-spirited.

"I thought you said you'd stay."

Scott looked up. His foot missed the pants leg and shot out straight. He fell backward, landing on his ass with a loud *thump*. His head smacked the bookcase behind him. He could hear the books shift above and expected a collection of them to fall onto him. They didn't, but he thought he felt a remnant of his cum drip onto his head. That had to be his imagination in overdrive.

Mark laughed, but he also had a concerned look on his face as he reached down to him. "Are you okay?"

Scott nodded, but the only thing he could say was, "Stay?"

"Yes." Mark gripped his forearm and helped him up. "Stay the night."

Scott looked at the apartment door, then to the hallway entrance on the opposite side of the room leading to Mark's bedroom. Mark couldn't mean stay to have sex again. Or maybe he did. Maybe this really was a porno. They'd had sex in a library, after all. Who did that? Had there been video cameras he missed? Mark's dark eyes were scanning his face. No. Mark would never do that. Scott wasn't sure why, but he trusted him. His dad had always said he had good instincts about people. "Stay?" he asked. "To sleep?"

"Yes. I thought we went over this already. Not all guys are assholes about the staying-over thing. Come on. You've got tomorrow for your homework, right?"

"Okay." He'd been overthinking everything, which probably made him look even more inexperienced. Maybe Mark hadn't noticed, or maybe he liked Scott just the way he was. Which would be the best part of such an unforgettable day. He didn't like worrying about whether he looked assertive enough or if he talked about football or action movies or typical "guy stuff" enough. He reached for his underwear and bent to put them on.

"What are you doing?" Mark gripped his arm again, stopping him as he held his underwear down by his shins.

Thank God he hadn't lifted a leg yet. The feeling of Mark's firm touch, so strong, unwavering, would've sent him tumbling backward again for sure. "Uh...I'm getting dressed."

"But we're heading to bed."

Right. He had to be missing something. He was bent over with Mark's hand on his forearm. A very naked Mark. Who wanted him to stay over but not to put his clothes on. Oh God. He *was* just a kid. "You want to sleep naked." He wished he could take back the words as soon as they'd left his mouth.

Mark let out another laugh. "Oh man, you're adorable."

Scott stood, the underwear still in his right hand. "You're making fun of me." Why did that hurt worse than anything the big jerk Gigantor had said to him at the library earlier?

"I'm sorry. I didn't mean to hurt your feelings. I wasn't making fun." He held Scott's face, this time in both hands. "I find you genuine and refreshing. Just be yourself." Mark slid the underwear from Scott's grip and tossed them over his shoulder. "Come on. I want to see you in my bed." He gripped Scott's hand and led the way.

Mark's words and their hands connected in such a simple touch gave Scott a confidence he didn't always feel. He could be himself. That was easy. He didn't know how people pretended to be anything else. Or why.

Maybe to get into bed with a guy like Mark.

He'd managed that without even trying. He couldn't hold back the smile.

The bedroom had bland off-white rental-apartment walls, with space barely big enough for the double bed, dresser, and end table. But none of that mattered. From the moment they stepped into the room all Scott cared to see was Mark pulling back the bedcovers, moving slowly, with determination, like he had all the time in the world to focus on the here and now. He was mesmerizing to watch. Scott pictured the very naked Mark tying him spread-eagle on the bed, using the red rope to secure his arms to the wooden posts at each end of the headboard.

Mark's voice snapped Scott from the fantasy. "This is the part where you lie down."

"Oh, okay." Scott crawled on hands and knees onto the bed, flopped over, and lay on his back. He expected to feel uncomfortable, nervous. He'd never spent the night with a man, never slept beside one. But all he felt was at ease, like he'd done this a thousand times before.

Mark got on the bed and moved in close beside him. He propped his head on his hand. "Do your wrists hurt?"

"No."

Mark ran a hand down Scott's bare chest and asked, "Have you been tied up a lot?"

"No. Most guys don't have the patience." Not that he'd ever asked any of them. Not that there'd been many to ask.

"Yeah. They're usually all about the fucking; then they head out the door as soon as it's over. I've been there."

"But I've done some—" He snapped his mouth shut.

"Solo bondage?"

"Yeah. But it's not the same."

Mark focused on his dragon tattoo again, tracing it with his thumb. "No, it's not." His hand stilled, and he looked up at Scott. "So what brought you here?"

"Here? In your bed?"

Mark smiled. He had eyes that almost closed when he smiled. Those eyes gave him the look of someone who had seen the truths of secrets no one else knew existed, like wisdom and amazement all in one look. Scott could get lost in that look. Too lost?

"To this school," Mark said.

"Oh. It was the closest university with a strong history program."

"Closest to what?"

"Home." He paused, then added, "Close to my dad."

"Where's home?"

"Elmore, Michigan. Just"—Scott sucked in a quick breath as Mark cupped his balls and caressed the sensitive skin behind them—"just north of the state line."

Mark ran his hand up Scott's body and laid a palm over his heart. "You're graduating this year?"

"Yeah."

"Then what are you going to do?"

"I've been accepted to Michigan State for their Master of Arts program in history."

"That's impressive."

"Thanks." One professor after another had commented on Scott's hard work and congratulated him on his acceptance, but those two words from Mark made him feel proud like nothing else had. "It's farther from home, but I'll still be close enough."

Mark nodded as if every word from Scott made perfect sense. Which seemed odd. They barely knew each other. Then he asked, "Close enough for what?"

Scott's confidence waned. *Be yourself.* He wanted to reach for the blankets Mark had folded down to the end of the bed. He felt even more naked than before.

"It's okay," Mark said. "You don't have to talk about it." He paused. "Your reading tastes are extensive. You seemed really into that comic book today. One of your favorites?"

He nodded. *Be yourself.* The words flowed easily this time. "I like the idea of being a superhero, having a secret identity. That you can be one person during the day—mild-mannered, quiet, smart—and still be something different when it matters. When someone needs you,

you can do the right thing and not let fear or weakness keep you from doing it."

Mark gave that knowing smile again. "I think I need to read more comic books."

Scott didn't give that too much thought. He couldn't. He might ask Mark if he had any interest in reading a graphic novel—one graphic novel in particular. A very bad idea. Instead he said, "You ask a lot of questions."

Another laugh surged out of Mark. "I guess I do. And usually you're the one with the questions."

Scott nodded. Another part of him that annoyed most guys.

"Okay." Mark removed his hand from Scott, sat up, and leaned back against the headboard. He clasped his hands behind his head. "Ask away. Anything you want."

Scott sat up and took in the sight of Mark's naked body all spread out beside him. "Can I touch you while I ask?"

Mark's nostrils flared on his next breath. "Please do."

Where to start? Scott touched a finger to Mark's mouth, slid it back and forth, lingering on the lips he'd kissed several times that day. He moved his hand lower to the firm pectoral muscles of Mark's chest. He brushed the tips of his fingers through the sexy patch of dark chest hair. Were Mark's nipples as sensitive as his? "When do you graduate?"

"This semester." Mark's upper body surged forward and he hissed as Scott tugged lightly on a nipple. Guess he had answers to two questions. Mark added, "I'm defending my dissertation soon."

Scott stilled his hand. So that was it. No way would this be anything long-term. He should get up and leave, but he couldn't stop himself. He asked, "What are you doing after school?"

"I'm in the final running for a couple of teaching positions in Seattle."

Washington. Teaching. More they didn't have in common. Scott stared at the headboard over Mark's shoulder. "I could never teach."

"Why not? You're damn smart, that's for sure."

Scott rolled away and lay flat on his back. "I don't do so good...you know, with people looking at me, watching me." Then why was he relaxed now? Mark was watching him, pretty intently too.

Without warning, Mark rolled on top of him.

Instinctively, like breathing, Scott spread his legs, and Mark settled between them, his weight pressing down on Scott's upper body.

"So what do you want to do when you're done with your

master's?" Mark asked.

"Write books. I mean, I write and do my own illustrations now, but I'd like to get paid for it someday." Scott hadn't even thought about it that time. He'd just answered. He hadn't told anyone other than his dad and Owen about his novels. Most people would probably laugh their asses off.

"You've written a book? With illustrations?" Mark didn't sound like he was going to laugh. "A children's book?"

"I've written three, but...they're not children's books."

"Fiction?"

"Yes."

"With illustrations?"

Scott tried to read the expression on Mark's face. He liked the wide-eyed wonder, so he squeezed his own eyes shut and said it. "They're graphic novels. Fantasy. You know...with magic, swords, and dragons."

There was a long silence. Then Mark asked, "You wrote all three during college?"

"Yes." Scott opened his eyes. Mark was smiling down at him. A sexy smile unlike any he'd flashed yet, and Scott lost his train of thought.

"You're something else," Mark said. "Have you tried to get them published?"

"Not yet. I entered one in a contest, though."

Mark sat up and straddled Scott's hips. "The Breakout Writer Award the school's hosting this year?"

"Yeah."

"That's awesome."

Scott liked the look on Mark's face, even liked lying naked in his bed, talking, sharing a part of himself that had nothing to do with sex.

This was such a bad idea. It wouldn't take long to get attached to Mark Lewis. And then what?

Falling for a guy had never been a good idea. Look what that had gotten him in the past—nothing. Look what love had gotten his dad—a life alone.

But another killer smile from Mark, and that was it. Scott was such a goner.

Chapter Three

Mark had no words. He just stared down at Scott. He couldn't help himself. Never had he met anyone this smart and sexy, so utterly inspiring. "You're pretty cool, you know that?"

Scott met his stare. "Me?"

"Hell yeah, you."

"Oh." Scott searched Mark's eyes. "Have you…" He looked away and shifted his ass between Mark's thighs.

"What?"

Scott stilled and met his gaze again. "Have you done this a lot?"

"Done what?" Mark moved to lie on his side beside Scott again, and Scott followed until they were face-to-face. The intimacy of being in bed with a guy long after the sex washed over Mark. This was crazy. He was usually the one coming on strong. Now it was Scott, with his curiosity and quiet, nervous charm, who was the one slamming into Mark's resolve to take this slow, to keep his emotions in check, or else he'd push Scott too far too fast. He didn't want to scare him off. He could come on strong, could be too intense for most guys.

Scott said, "Bring men home you barely know."

"Sometimes." None of them had been this interesting, this meaningful, not on a first date. He kept that to himself.

Scott's brow furrowed, and then, in a swift move, he turned onto his back.

Shit. That look. Hurt? Confused? Mark didn't want Scott to misunderstand. What they'd done at the library and again at his apartment was special—damn special. But yet again, he held back from saying too much. Not now. Not yet. He sat up and leaned against the headboard. "I'm not all about getting laid. It's just sometimes I meet someone, and I bring him home."

"Of course." Scott sat up and turned away, his legs swinging off the side of the bed. "I get it. I mean, I know I'm weird. Not going out that much…not sleeping around."

"That's not weird." Mark couldn't hold back on all of it. "It's been a long time since I've wanted anyone to stay in bed with me. Since I've wanted to talk with a guy."

Scott turned. "But you're talking to me."

"Yeah. That's the difference with you."

Scott cocked his head to the side, not as animated as before, but he was still staring with an openness that called to Mark. "Difference?"

"I want to get to know you. I'd like to see you again."

Scott pulled one leg onto the bed and turned toward him. "Yeah?"

Mark hesitated. This could be more than he'd let himself hope for with any man. More than he was ready to put himself on the line for. So far Scott was proving he was worth the chance. Even with only the possibility of four months. "Yeah."

"That…that would be—" Scott stood. "I don't know how to—I should go." He glanced around the room, his head jerking side to side so quickly he'd give himself whiplash if he didn't let up. "Where are my pants?"

Mark sat up. "Living room. Scott, what's wrong?"

Scott rounded the foot of the bed and headed for the door. Mark reached out, needing to stop him. He missed Scott's arm, almost falling off the bed with the stretch, and Scott kept on going into the hall.

"Wait. Scott." He jumped out of the bed and dashed after him. How the hell had he managed to fuck this up already?

In the living room, Scott was putting on his pants. "My shirt?" Before Mark had a chance to say anything, Scott found his T-shirt. He slipped it over his head and grabbed his backpack. The shirt was still rolled up around his chest as he pulled the pack onto his shoulder.

"Scott." There was a fine line between sounding like an ass and using a firm voice with a submissive man. Many of the guys who took the role of a sub in the bedroom didn't want to do so anywhere else. Scott had responded so well to Mark's instructions at the library before they'd even gotten their clothes off. Would he run from his requests now?

Scott stopped before he reached the apartment door. His body went still. Slowly, in an exaggerated move that was both unsure and tense, he faced Mark.

"Come here."

He walked to him. Slow, uneasy, but still doing what Mark asked.

"I'm sorry," Scott said when he stood before Mark.

"What are you sorry for?"

He wouldn't meet Mark's gaze. His lower lip trembled. "I can't do this." He rushed to the apartment door and threw it open.

No way. Their time together was not ending like this. With no explanation. Not when Mark wasn't sure what he'd done to scare Scott. Or maybe to hurt him.

Mark lunged for the open door but stopped one step into the hall when he spotted his neighbor and her four-year-old daughter at the far end. He couldn't afford to get kicked out of his building for running down the hall naked.

He headed back in and wrangled on his pants. When he made his way into the hall again, there was no sign of Scott. Mark took the stairs two at a time, his bare feet slipping on the worn, cheap carpet, sending him sliding down the last four steps. The rug burn on the soles of his feet didn't stop him. He sprinted through the small entranceway and shoved open the glass door. A pebble jabbed into the bottom of his right foot, and the bare toes on his other foot scraped the concrete sidewalk as he tripped forward. He hobbled down the sidewalk to the corner of his street, looking one way, then the other.

Scott was nowhere in sight.

"Fuck." He bent forward and clenched his knees in his hands as he caught his breath. So much for slowing things down and not freaking Scott out. "Fuck!" He'd royally screwed that up. And he wasn't even sure how he'd done it.

* * *

Scott hit refresh on his e-mail's inbox.

Nothing.

He really needed to shut his laptop lid and quit checking every five minutes. It was only lunchtime. He was going to drive himself nuts at this rate. For all he knew, the announcement about the finalists wouldn't come out until later that night.

He reached for the bottle of Mountain Dew sitting beside him on the small table in the back of the coffee shop and chugged down a series of long gulps as he tried to find his place in the book he'd been reading. The latest novel by Dean Koontz. He wanted to finish the other book from the night before but no way could he carry that around campus with him. He should have bought it as an e-book so he could read it on his laptop and not have to worry about comments from people who couldn't figure out how to mind their own business. But he loved this author. He always got the print version of her releases to add to his collection. He couldn't afford to buy both formats, and it wasn't like the university library carried that kind of book.

"How's the cake?" Owen was walking toward him from the front of the coffee shop. Scott hadn't even seen him come out of the kitchen.

The place was crowded. Like usual. The small round wooden tables, low lighting from floor and table lamps as opposed to the typical overhead fluorescent lighting in the school dining hall, and the upholstered chairs scattered throughout the restaurant gave the place a relaxed, homey feel. It was that atmosphere that attracted students from the crowded dorms and shabby apartments all over campus and the surrounding city blocks. With a cappuccino and a laptop, most students could get lost for hours in Owen's place. It also didn't hurt that Owen let them plug in their devices and stay as long as they wanted, provided they ordered one thing off the menu. Even if that one thing was the cheapest coffee he served and included free refills.

Scott smiled at Owen and answered his question about the cake. "Good. Lots of frosting." He grabbed his fork and took another bite to demonstrate the irresistible taste. Truth was, he'd forgotten he had the slice of chocolate cake sitting beside him.

"Just the way you like it," the bulky gray-haired man said with a laugh as he stopped to stand on the other side of Scott's table.

Owen was always teasing Scott about the amount of sugar he consumed. Which was fine by Scott. He liked Owen, considered the man a friend, probably his best friend—either on or off campus—who wasn't someone he chatted with online in one of the comic book forums. Owen had been running Not Just Java long before Scott had first started coming in to the coffee shop his freshman year. Owen spent his days serving hot drinks with complicated names that included more sugary syrups than coffee. Before that, he'd run three other establishments in the same location. He'd changed the restaurant's business model each time he started to lose money, keeping up with the shift in the college-aged consumers' interests.

That was another reason Scott liked him. Owen was smart. He also reminded Scott of his father, with the chef's apron and wide smile. During Scott's youth, his dad had always worn an apron in the kitchen as he'd made dinner, washed dishes, or baked a cake for Scott's birthday or cookies for the annual bake sale at school or whenever he'd felt like making something sweet for Scott. His dad had done it all with a smile and not one complaint.

Hanging out in Not Just Java felt like being home.

It was almost as good as the library. In the coffee shop, most everyone sat at tables and the upholstered chairs, bent over their laptops or e-book readers. He could sit there, away from his loud roommates, and feel like he was hanging out, having the college experience. He could also disappear into his own world as he read or wrote or drew his latest sketches.

"Any news yet?" Owen asked.

"Not yet." Scott glanced out the wall of windows at the front of the shop. The sign announcing the Breakout Writer Convention was stretched across the main street that headed through campus. The plastic sign flapped in the wind, and with no sound to go with the movement, it was like watching a muted TV. A surreal effect that matched how out of sorts he felt.

He just wasn't sure if it was waiting to hear news about the writing competition that had him all messed up. Or the day before with Mark Lewis.

Scott couldn't believe he'd actually done it. Slept with a guy he'd just met. And not just once. Twice. And not just at the guy's apartment. In the library.

When the last man he'd been with over two years ago had used him and dumped him after only one week, he swore he'd never do casual sex again. No matter how horny he was. No matter how few and far between the offers came.

Owen patted his shoulder. "You'll hear soon. And I have a feeling we'll be celebrating this time tomorrow."

Scott focused on Owen again. "Thanks. I know it's a long shot."

"Hey, I made the money to buy this place betting on long shots at the track. It only takes one win. Then you'll have your foot in the door."

True. But it would suck to get his hopes up. Or were they already? "Yeah."

Owen gave another pat to his shoulder and returned to the kitchen through the doorway beside Scott's table.

The front door to the coffee shop flew open and loud giggles poured in with the menagerie of girls who entered. Scott jumped with the explosion of high-pitched chatter. His forearm smacked into the Mountain Dew bottle. It went sailing into the cake, smearing the chocolate frosting along one side of the soda bottle, the Dew spilling all over the table and splashing on the empty chair across from him.

He really needed to calm down. It was just one competition. It didn't mean the end of his writing career.

He grabbed napkins and started cleaning up the mess. Then he stopped. It had been a couple of minutes since he last checked. With the napkins crumpled into a ball in his fist and his fingers still covered in frosting, he smeared the chocolate onto his laptop's touchpad as he hit the refresh button on his e-mail.

Nothing.

Ignoring the frosting growing sticky on his computer, he clicked over to the competition's website and hit refresh.

Nothing.

Resolved to another few minutes of not knowing, he returned to cleaning up the chocolate Dew concoction.

It was ridiculous to be so nervous. Even if he didn't win, he had no intention of giving up on his writing or drawing.

Then why was he so anxious?

Because this was not some local competition. This was a national award that just happened to be hosted at the university this year. The winner received a meeting with one of the sponsoring publishers. This was a chance at a publishing contract.

He'd come a long way since that first comic he'd created in high school. The one his dad had found hidden under his bed.

The next morning after that discovery had been one of the hardest moments of his life. Without a word his dad had sat across from him at the kitchen table and slid over the comic with its gay superhero and equally gay sidekick who were falling for each other. Thank God he hadn't even considered writing something as erotic as the comic he'd seen in the popular culture library the day before. Although it didn't matter that there was no sex in the one he'd created. The gay love story was obvious.

Turned out his dad had always suspected Scott was gay, and finding the comic poking out from under the mattress while collecting laundry in Scott's room had given him the perfect opening. "Anything you want to tell me?" he asked, then quickly added, "I promise I won't freak out."

So Scott had told him everything. About how he'd felt like he couldn't fit in all through junior high school, knowing he was different than the other boys in his small twenty-kids-per-grade private school. About the boy he'd met his last year at band camp. The one who'd given him his first kiss. About the gay fiction he'd been secretly buying off the Internet for weeks before his dad found the comic. Scott had reassured his dad he wasn't sleeping around. He wanted a boyfriend, a relationship. After twenty minutes of nonstop talking, Scott took a deep breath and sat back in the kitchen chair.

"Well, I want to meet him when you do," his dad had said. Then he'd given him a smile. "I'm glad you could be honest with me. I love you, Scott. Not just because you're my son. I love the person you are. Exactly as you are. Never doubt that."

Then he'd proceeded to lecture Scott about safer sex, including a demonstration on how to put a condom on a banana. After the demo, he'd made Scott do it on his own. Three times. When Scott finally got up from the table to toss the condoms in the trash, he could feel the burn of embarrassment on his face.

Despite that, he'd never loved his dad more than in that moment.

His dad didn't ask every time they talked, but he did ask from time to time if Scott had met someone. It wasn't hard to miss the worry in the question. His dad had spent a lot of years alone since he lost his wife. He'd never remarried. Never talked about anyone special. Never even brought a date home.

And six years since his dad had found that gay comic hidden under his mattress, Scott still hadn't brought anyone home to meet his dad.

He'd be disappointed to know that Scott had met a guy at the library and less than an hour later had been pressed face-first on a table with the guy's dick plowing his ass. And even more disappointed to know Scott had considered spending more time with Mark, a man who would never be more than a four-month fuck.

Scott finished cleaning up the sticky mess on his laptop and the table, then returned to the book he'd been reading. On the third read of the same paragraph, he gave up. He really should head to the library and do some research for his History of Ancient Greece class.

He couldn't avoid the library forever.

But he could avoid it on the day after he'd made a fool of himself with Mark Lewis.

If not longer than one day.

Maybe a week.

Or two.

Better to stick with online research for now.

He must have looked ridiculous and immature storming out of Mark's apartment like that. Now even the fantasies would be tainted by that embarrassment.

But the sex—oh man, he'd never felt so alive. So cared for. Mark was just the kind of guy he'd been dreaming about. A guy who was smart and confident. A guy who could fuck like no one Scott had ever been with. Or dreamed of being with. A guy who took the reins and didn't make Scott feel weak for letting him—or for wanting him to.

A guy who was into sports and who was leaving to head across the country at the end of the semester.

Did they have anything in common besides books and sex? Why

had Mark asked him to sleep over? Why had he told Scott he wanted to get to know him?

This had to stop. Scott was done thinking about what he couldn't have.

That was why he'd spent the night engrossed in a stack of books. To keep from remembering the way Mark had touched him, the way he'd looked at him. The way he had bound him to the bookcase with the red rope and used the tie to blindfold him.

Scott had read until he couldn't keep his eyes open any longer. Which was good because he could tell the last book he'd been reading was leading to a long, emotional sex scene. He would never have made it through that without thinking of Mark.

Maybe it was a good thing he'd left that book at home. He should keep reading the Koontz one he'd brought with him. Anything to make the waiting easier, to forget about the writing competition. And the day before. To forget about the chance of having everything he'd dreamed of for years and not having the choice of whether he got it or not.

He stared at the banner hanging across the street. So much for not thinking about Mark Lewis and what had happened the day before. Because there, walking across the street directly under the sign announcing the Breakout Writer Convention, was Gigantor, the guy Mark had kicked out of the library.

Gigantor was talking with two other guys. Fellow football players by the looks of them. They continued across the street and walked by the entrance of the coffee shop. Curiosity hit Scott. Like it always did. About everything. He pulled up the school's website and browsed to the athletic pages. He scanned through the current photos of the football players. Under the section titled *Team Captains* was Gigantor, aka Bruce Kreger. Apparently Bruce played football well. Really well. He was on a four-year scholarship and was featured in over half the articles on the site about this year's team.

Scott closed the school's page and found himself staring at the contest's webpage again.

It had to have been five minutes since he last checked. He hit refresh on the browser window, and his breath caught.

There it was. The list of finalists.

He scrolled to the Graphic Novel category.

Holy shit. "Holy shit!"

He flung his hand over his mouth to shut himself up.

Owen popped his head out from around the corner of the kitchen doorway, a towel in his wet hands. "Yeah?"

Laughter surged out of Scott. "Yeah."

Owen was beside his table, patting his back and checking out the list of finalists over Scott's shoulder before he could stop laughing.

He couldn't believe it. He flipped to his e-mail and there it was. A message letting him know his novel, *The Hawk in the Caverns*, had been selected as a finalist. Included in the message was the list of instructions for the next phase of the competition. He'd have until the convention later that semester to make any revisions to the story or the art based on the first-round judges' comments.

"This is wonderful," Owen said. "Congratulations, Scott. You come by tomorrow and lunch is on me."

"Thanks."

Owen flipped the towel over his shoulder and backed away from the table. "I'll let you call your dad. Don't tell him I knew before him." He winked and headed into the kitchen again.

Scott grabbed his phone and made the call. No answer. Which was weird. His dad always kept his phone with him wherever he went. Scott stared at the screen on his phone. There was no one else to call.

It was nice to be able to share this with Owen and eventually his dad, but it would be even better to have someone special to celebrate with. Someone like Mark. Someone he could share more than sex with. Someone he could share everything with, every day.

Now how ridiculous did he sound? That was more than almost anyone his age was looking for.

He returned to his e-mail and read the list of comments from the judges. Most of them loved the story and the art, but almost all made comments about the ending. That it had fallen flat in comparison to the rest of the story. It needed something, only no one was specific in the comments about what it needed.

He couldn't imagine how he could rework the ending. He'd have to give that some thought.

Later. He'd worry about it after the excitement wore off. Right now, he wanted to enjoy the success. He gave another look at the list of finalists. He couldn't hold back the smile. Or the little dance. Right there in a chair at the back of the coffee shop, he celebrated on his own.

Eventually, when his cheeks were sore from the smiling and he'd read the e-mail four more times, he picked up the book he'd been reading and stuffed it and his laptop in his bag. He headed out the front of the coffee shop and almost missed the groans and the sharp *slap* of a fist slamming against flesh. Then he saw them. Two men at the far end of the alleyway between Not Just Java and the convenience store next door. One man was bent over the other, pummeling the one on the ground. Despite the dark alleyway, Scott could see it was Bruce Kreger slamming his fists into the other man's face.

Scott turned to run back into the shop. He'd get Owen, they'd call the police, and—

"You regret it yet, asshole?" Bruce's words sounded as if they were forced out through clenched teeth. Beyond anger. Furious.

"Never."

That voice.

It was Mark.

Scott faced the two men again. Instinctively, without a thought on what he'd do when he reached them, he dropped his bag and sprinted down the alley.

As he got closer, the dark shadows of the two men gave way to more vivid details. Mark was lying on the ground, half his face covered in blood. He had an arm over his head, using his forearm to block the punches. With a flurry of jabs, Bruce was pounding on him, or trying to. It looked like he'd already given his best effort, and now more of his swings were missing their mark than were making contact.

Scott called out, "Leave him alone!" Almost there. With another couple of pumps of his legs he'd reach Mark. And Gigantor. Football star Bruce Kreger. A guy who could break Scott's face with one punch.

This was why he usually gave his actions more thought before jumping into something.

Bruce was no longer hammering on Mark but was facing Scott. "You want a piece of this?"

Scott pulled to a stop. "No. I want you to leave him alone."

"Don't," Mark said. He had a hand pressed to his head above his left eye, trying to stanch the blood from a cut by the look of the streaks of red running down his cheek. He was working to a standing position, inching his way up the brick wall behind him. "Get out of here, Scott." That must have been all he could manage right then. He teetered and fell back to his ass.

Bruce laughed. "Leave it to a fag to need his weakling sissy boyfriend to rescue him." Bruce rubbed at his jaw with the back of his hand. He had a bruise forming. And a cut on his upper lip. There was another bruise over his eye in the same location where Mark had his hand above his eye. How long had they been out here fighting?

The stillness of the air in the narrow alley between brick buildings and the quietness of that same space faded in an instant when Bruce charged forward. Scott held his ground. He wouldn't give this bully the satisfaction. Bruce grabbed him by the collar of his T-shirt with two hands and hauled him against the wall of the convenience store, Scott's back hitting the brick hard and knocking the breath from his chest. The scratchy surface scraped along his skin through his shirt as he slid down the wall. His feet finally found the ground beneath him. Bruce still had a hold of his shirt, and Scott gripped Bruce's forearms in both hands.

"The two of you are pathetic, you know that?" Bruce spat the words in an exaggerated, enraged tone. A spray of spit landed on Scott's cheek. Without letting up on the grip of one hand, Bruce pointed toward the end of the alley where Scott had come from. "I saw you lookin' at that sign. What's it for? That writin' competition? You think you can win something like that? What a joke. Even those book geeks are going to laugh at you."

"You might as well let me go. I'm not going to fight you."

"That's not a surprise. Guys like you always take the chickenshit way out."

"I'm not going to run. I'm going to see if Mark's okay."

"Not if I stop you first."

"By hitting me? You know, only people who aren't smart enough to figure out something better, use their fists to get what they want."

That did it. He really needed to think before he spoke, because Bruce had a clenched fist raised in the air.

"Bruce!" Two men stood at the end of the alley. His friends from earlier with plastic carryout bags in their hands. "Come on. We're late," the tallest one said. "Leave him alone. He's just a little guy. We've got practice."

"You should let me go," Scott said. "You're not even scoring points with your own buddies."

Yep, Scott really needed to shut his mouth. Bruce's grip tightened, and he had both hands back holding Scott against the wall.

Somehow Scott couldn't shut himself up. "No matter what you do to me, you're the ass here, not me. I can live with that."

In a rush Bruce let go of Scott and took a step back. The corners of his mouth turned up. "Why, you little shit, you're tougher than you look."

Maybe this was how you earned a guy like Bruce's respect. Scott tugged his shirt down from where Bruce had balled it up at the collar in his fists.

"This is stupid," his friend called out. "We're leaving." His voice trailed off as he and the other guy walked out of view at the end of the alley.

"They're just leaving you?" Scott asked. "Those are some great friends you've got."

Bruce grabbed Scott's shirt again and opened his mouth to speak. He didn't get out a sound. Mark crashed into his side, detangling Bruce's grip on Scott. Both Mark and Bruce slammed to the ground, Mark half on top. He scrambled to kneeling and straddled Bruce's legs. He shoved the side of Bruce's face against the dirt. Then Bruce did a gyration of his hips under Mark that would've made any gay man proud. They rolled on the dirt, over and over, one man gaining dominance for a moment, and then their positions reversed again.

Scott circled them, looking for a time and place to intervene. He should've done more fighting as a kid. Or paid attention when the other boys got into it. What kind of a grown man didn't know how to jump into the battle, either to become a part of it or to pull them apart?

"What the hell is going on here?" Owen was jogging down the alleyway toward them. "You boys break it up."

They either hadn't heard Owen or had no plans to comply.

Owen stopped beside Scott, and without so much as a move toward the brawling men, he had a handle of the situation. "Break it up or I'm calling the cops."

That got Bruce's attention. He let up from where he had Mark on his stomach, eating dirt. Bruce stared up at Owen for a long, considering moment. Then he gave one last good shove to the side of Mark's face. "Don't you fuckin' come at me again." He leaned forward and spat on him. The glob of saliva landed on Mark's cheek and dripped between his nose and mouth. Bruce got off him and casually walked by Scott and Owen as if he was heading to class and it didn't matter that his clothes and face were sweat-soaked with dirt caked to the moisture, forming a paste on his pale skin.

Scott dropped beside Mark and carefully helped him roll onto his back. "Are you all right?" He reached forward to touch Mark's face, then pulled back, too afraid he'd hurt him more than he already was.

"Do you know him?" Owen asked, gesturing to Mark.

"We sort of had a date. I mean, I think it was a date. Well, maybe not." Scott felt his cheeks flush, and he focused on Mark again. The blood on his face was now smeared with dirt and spit, making him look more like Bruce had than Scott cared to think about.

"It was a date." Mark spoke the words through gritted teeth as he met Scott's gaze. There was earnestness and compassion in those dark eyes visible amid the blood and grime covering his face.

"I see," Owen said. "Let me get my keys, and we'll drive him to the hospital."

"No." Mark sat up. He slowly eased his legs around and got onto his knees.

Scott wrapped an arm around his waist. "Let me help you."

"I'm okay." Despite his words Mark leaned his weight against Scott, and together they got him to a standing position. "I just need to get to my place."

"You need to see a doctor." Scott's stomach churned at the thought of pushing Mark on anything, but he had to say something. "And you need to call the police about Bruce."

"I can't." Mark met his gaze. With Scott's arm around him and Mark's height reduced by his inability to stand upright, their heads—and lips—were close. That had a shiver working its way down Scott's body. So did Mark's next words. "I'm the one who started the fight."

* * *

Mark let his eyes fall shut and leaned his hip against the hall wall beside his apartment door. God, he hurt. Everywhere.

"Mark, are you okay?"

He opened his eyes, and there was Scott, his brow furrowed and his gaze unwavering. He looked frustrated and worried. And maybe scared. Not a look Mark ever wanted to see in those eyes. Not after the desire and lust and passion he'd witnessed on Scott's face the day before. He should tell him to leave. Scott was probably only there out of some twisted obligation because Mark had fucked him.

"I'm okay. I'm sorry you saw me like that. In the alley." He must've looked out of control when he was battling Bruce. Like an asshole. A crazed, feral brute. Worse than that…he hated how Scott had looked at him after he confessed his part in starting the fight.

"I was scared he was going to hurt you. I mean, more than he did." Scott kept a steadying hand on Mark's arm as he unlocked the door. He looked good opening the door to Mark's apartment. Just not for the reason they were there. He wanted Scott walking into his place again because of choice—and desire—not because Scott felt he had to.

Mark leaned his hip and shoulder harder against the wall, wishing he could slip right through the plaster and paint to get inside without Scott needing to give him one more hand with the simple task of walking. He ignored the disappointment when his body didn't ooze through the wall. He said, "I forgot to thank Owen for the ride and the help up the stairs." Owen had driven them to the hospital, then waited with Scott until he could drive them to Mark's place. When they'd gotten up the stairs to his floor, Scott had insisted he could get them the rest of the way to the apartment. Mark wasn't sure if it was out of embarrassment that Owen would see them together for one moment more or so they could be alone. He was hoping for the latter, even if he didn't want to face telling Scott about what he'd done in that alley. Or why.

"It's okay," Scott said as he swung the apartment door in. "Owen was glad to help."

"Tell him thanks for me later?"

"Of course." Scott wrapped his arm around Mark's waist and eased him away from the wall. "Easy. Let's get you inside."

"I just need to get to the bathroom, then rest for a bit. You don't have to help me anymore."

Scott didn't let go of him. "I'm not leaving you alone like this." He set his bag by the door, then moved them through the living room and down the short hall to the bathroom.

It took Mark's eyes a moment to adjust to the glare of the overhead bathroom light fixture that somehow seemed brighter than even the hospital's lights had. He shuffled to the sink and got a good look in the mirror. The dried blood and clumps of dirt he'd seen in the rearview mirror of Owen's car on the drive to the hospital were gone. Now there was no missing the black eye, the stitched and bandaged cut above his other eye, or the bruising on the opposite cheek and all along his jawline. His hands were equally bruised with bandages covering several of the knuckles. Not a pretty sight. Not how he pictured his next meeting with Scott.

"Here." Scott slipped behind him and raised the lid and seat on the toilet.

Mark could manage taking a piss on his own. Too bad moving around, even in the small space of his bathroom, didn't sound too good. He didn't protest when Scott helped him to the toilet and proceeded to unbuckle his belt. Then it all sank in...what he was letting him do. "Scott."

"Don't." Scott was shaking his head.

"Don't what?"

"Don't talk like that. In that tone. Not now." He moved away from Mark and looked through the medicine cabinet beside the mirror, taking out bandages, a roll of gauze, and a tube of antibiotic cream. Mark relieved himself and tucked his prick back into his briefs, leaving his jeans open.

Scott was setting the items he'd found on the counter. "Looks like you have enough supplies when it's time to change the bandage." He faced Mark again. He looked nervous. More nervous than Mark had seen yet. Even when he'd first walked up to the table where Scott was sitting in the library reading the comic.

"I'm staying," Scott added. "And I'm going to help you."

"Okay."

"You don't have to be embarrassed. Or feel weak about someone wanting to help you."

Sounded like something Mark would've said. He breathed deep, and his side hurt with the action. He held back the wince. "Okay."

Scott moved to stand in the doorway while Mark stepped to the sink. Before he could finish washing his hands, Scott spoke again.

"Why did you do it?" It was almost a whisper.

Mark faced him, but Scott wouldn't meet his gaze. Mark didn't want to talk about this, but he couldn't avoid the question, didn't want Scott to feel like he couldn't talk if he needed to, that he couldn't ask questions.

"It was a mistake. I reacted without thinking."

"Because of what happened at the library yesterday?"

"No, because of what Bruce did today."

Scott finally looked at him. "What did he do?"

Mark took a step closer. "He and his friends were watching you through the window of Not Just Java. He was talking shit about you."

"Oh."

"When his friends stepped into the carryout next door, I shoved him into the alley and gave him a piece of my mind. When he still wouldn't shut up, I…"

"You hit him."

"Yeah."

Scott looked disappointed. Damn, that stung.

"Are you hurt anywhere other than your hands and face?"

"Don't you want to know what he said?" Because Mark would never forget it. Never forget Bruce's words, or the hatred aimed at Scott.

"Disgusting, faggot. He's never met a real man. If he had a real piece of thick meat shoved up his ass, it'd split him open and he'd never beg for a guy to fuck him again. That's what all fairies like him need. Someone to rape and beat the fag out of them."

"I don't want to know," Scott said. "I don't care what guys like him think of me. Are you hurt anywhere else?"

"Just sore."

"Where?"

"My side."

Scott came closer and gripped the bottom of Mark's shirt. "Take this off. Let me see."

Having Scott physically care for him had Mark's stomach in knots. Had him feeling weak just like Scott had guessed. But the knowledge that Scott wanted to do it almost worked away the unease. Mark pulled his shirt over his head and said, "I didn't know you were so bossy."

Scott chuckled. It was a good sound. "You don't know that much about me."

He knew a lot but definitely not enough.

Scott ran his warm fingers along Mark's abs to his side. "There's a few bruises. Did they check this out at the hospital?"

"Yes. It's fine. The punches below the neck weren't that bad. He mostly hit my face."

"I can see that." Scott reached up and ran his thumb just below the split skin on Mark's lower lip.

That made it official. The unease was gone. At least about Scott taking care of him, touching him. Not about the reason they were alone in his apartment again. "Why did you leave last night?"

Scott stepped to the sink and lined up the medical supplies into a neat row near the back of the countertop, a slight shake in his hands as he worked. "I thought you were too good to be true."

That had Mark laughing. "I'm just a guy. One who makes mistakes."

Scott's gaze landed on Mark's split lip again. He gave a nod. "I get that. I thought I'd say or do something wrong." His voice dropped lower, a stiffness to his words Mark hadn't yet heard. "If we go out, spend time together, I might... I could fall for you."

Mark moved in and pressed his body against Scott's back and ass. "What makes you think I won't fall right back?"

That had Scott shaking his head. "I've never really dated anyone. Not someone I liked this much."

Mark watched him in the mirror over Scott's shoulder. "You are now."

The head tilt was back as Scott studied Mark's reflection. Maybe he liked what he saw. He smiled and nodded. "Yeah."

"Good. I'd like to take you out for dinner. Maybe catch a movie." Mark laughed again, the tension completely working its way from his body in a rush. "Not tonight, though."

"No, not tonight." Scott smiled again. He turned, slipped his arm around Mark's waist, and helped him to the bedroom.

Standing before the bed, Scott shimmied Mark's jeans down his legs, then knelt before him as he worked the jeans lower. When he had them bunched around Mark's calves, he looked up. This time he didn't speak. He waited. Maybe it was their proximity to the bed. Maybe it was that Scott really didn't like telling someone else— telling Mark—what to do, not even when he was taking care of him.

Mark cupped Scott's cheek in his hand, then dropped the hand to his shoulder and held on as he lifted each foot out of his shoes and then his pants. His muscles were stiff, as if he'd spent a week doing hard labor. Or fucking like mad. He left his briefs on and got into the bed, the sheets cool and inviting against his battered body. Even if Bruce hadn't hit him as hard as he could've below the neck, the blunt punches to his abs and side had left some damage in their wake.

"I'll be right back." Scott left the room and returned less than a minute later with a hard-back chair from Mark's living room. He placed the chair next to the bed and sat, a concerned look on his face again. Mark could only imagine how the slow, drawn-out movements of his slide into the bed must've looked. Especially in contrast to how confident and assured he'd been during what they'd done the day before.

"What are you doing in that chair? Get in bed with me." His instincts wanted to make it sound like a demand, but instead he forced playfulness to his tone. They weren't about to get into anything close to sex.

Scott stood and moved to the bed on the side opposite Mark. He pulled back the blankets and sheet and started to get in.

"Your shirt first."

"Oh." Scott straightened and tugged the shirt over his head. He dropped it to the floor.

"Now your shoes and socks."

He bent and removed them, then stood straight again.

"Your pants."

When he was down to only his underwear, he waited beside the bed, his breathing slow and even, relaxed. It was a beautiful sight. Both Scott's body and his desire—his need—to do what Mark wanted. Scott appeared calmer in this moment than he had since he found Mark in the alley. Maybe holding back on their instincts wasn't a good idea. For either of them.

"Climb in," Mark said, and Scott did, sliding under the sheet until they were both covered to their waists. They were facing each other, Mark lying on his least-bruised side, Scott's hands folded together and tucked under his cheek on the pillow.

Everything shifted for Mark then. Scott looked innocent and lost. Like a boy who wasn't sure if he was doing the right thing. Maybe being this close to the bruises had him remembering what he'd seen in the alleyway.

Mark never wanted to be the kind of guy who had trouble keeping his anger in check, who could scare someone like Scott.

"Talk to me." He needed a connection with Scott. Something that wasn't about sex.

"About what?" Scott asked.

"About you. Tell me something...important to you. Something you've never shared with anyone else."

Scott was quiet for several moments. So long Mark feared he really had pushed too far too fast. Then Scott squeezed his eyes shut and whispered, "I killed my mom." He shook his head several times; then his eyes flew open. The sadness in those large, wide eyes hurt Mark worse than the beating from Bruce, worse than knowing his own anger and rash action had scared Scott.

"I know I didn't actually do it. I know it wasn't my fault, but it feels like that sometimes."

"What happened?" When Scott didn't say anything, Mark added, "Tell me."

"She died the night I was born. She was gone before I took my first breath. She never even saw me. And my dad's been alone ever since."

Mark had never been so moved by anyone's words.

Forget the sex. Scott needed him in ways that had nothing to do with sexual dominance or bondage or pleasure. Letting his instincts take over, he reached out and held Scott's face in his hands. "He wasn't alone. He had you."

Scott nodded, the sadness lifting as he gave a slight smile. "Tell me something important to you. Something you've never told anyone."

Chapter Four

This was not Mark's thing. He never shared anything too personal. Not even Dale had known much about his past, his dreams, or his fears.

But Scott had taken a leap of faith. Time to offer the same.

"I'm afraid of hurting someone." He paused, then forced himself to go on. "Of hurting you."

"Me? You mean..." Scott stiffened. He sat up in a flash. "I'm a grown man. I can take care of myself. I may not date much, but I'm not stupid. I know this isn't going to be a long-term thing."

"That's not what I meant." Mark swallowed hard and tried to keep his voice even. "I like to be in control, but I seem to be having a hard time doing that with you. The last guy who got under my skin in ways that had nothing to do with sex... Well, that ended badly, and it was all my fault."

"Relationships end badly or they wouldn't end."

"But this wasn't about the two of us no longer having feelings for each other. I hurt him." He rolled onto his back and winced when a stab of pain tore through his side. Where was the strong, confident man he'd been in the library? That's what Scott needed. Not this bruised, scared chickenshit. "Fuck. Let's just get some sleep."

Scott slid down to lie beside him again. A few minutes passed. Their breathing blended in the otherwise silence of the room. Scott whispered his next words into the space between them. "Did you say something that hurt him?"

"No."

"Did you cheat?"

"No!" Regret landed in Mark's gut the minute he snapped the word out.

Scott surged up again and turned to sit on the edge of the bed, his back to Mark. "Maybe I should go." His voice was shaky, his body held tight as he sat there. Waiting for Mark to say more? Or for the courage to walk out the door? Which was funny. Considering how much courage he'd shown running at Bruce in that alleyway.

Mark forced himself to speak. "Stay." He shouldn't have brought this up, but now he had to offer more. "I took things too far. Dale said he wanted more intense bondage, said he'd done it with other guys, but he told me later that wasn't true. He'd said that because he knew it was what I wanted. I was so far gone into the moment, I hadn't bothered to notice how uncomfortable he was. Before I could get the ropes off, he panicked and got hurt. Physically."

Scott spun around. "That's not your fault. He's the one who lied."

"That sounds good in theory." Mark scrubbed his face with both hands, wincing again when his finger caught the split lip. "God, I don't want to talk about this. Can we just sleep?"

Scott eased back down to the bed, and Mark reached out to pull him in close until Scott's head was lying on his chest. Scott tensed in his arms. "You're hurt."

"I'm good."

"Okay." Scott relaxed against him.

When was the last time Mark had held a man like this? That night with Dale. Thank God Scott wasn't shaking the way Dale had been.

Another long pause, and Scott said, "I won't lie to you."

Mark ran a hand down his bare back. He wanted to get closer, somehow touch more. "Thank you."

Scott relaxed even more as he slid his palm over Mark's chest. "I like the way you feel."

"Same here."

Scott lifted his head and placed one soft kiss after another across Mark's chest, then an even softer brush of lips down his bruised side and back up. "I've liked everything you've done to me."

Arousal and the need to take charge slammed into Mark. With the way his body ached, he wasn't getting hard anytime soon, but he couldn't resist doing one thing. He grabbed a fistful of Scott's hair and tugged until he met his stare. "What *we* did *together*."

Scott nodded, his breathing coming out in heavy pants. "You always know what to do. It's like you're inside my head."

"But I'm not. I've made some lucky guesses, did what I liked, and it happened to work out. I need to know you'll stop me if I do something you don't want."

"I will. I promise."

Mark let go and held him close again. He waited a moment, but he couldn't avoid one other topic. "Promise me something else."

Scott stared up at him, his chin resting on Mark's chest, those wide eyes so open and curious.

"What you did in that alley was incredibly brave, but I want you to keep clear of Bruce Kreger. He's a homophobic ass."

Scott looked away, a veil of sadness falling over his features. He traced an invisible line down Mark's chest with his forefinger like he needed something else to focus on. "I think he's gay."

"Yeah, me too." Mark should've known Scott was smart enough to pick up on that. "And he hates what he's feeling. Which is why you have to stay away from him." He paused, unsure if he should say the words, but Scott needed to hear them. "He said someone needed to rape and beat the fag out of you."

"Oh God." Scott trembled against him. "Do you think he meant he should do it?"

"Maybe." Mark didn't want to think about that. He'd give just about anything to forget this entire day. He wanted to roll Scott over onto his back and fuck him like crazy. Tie him down and make him fly. Give Scott what he needed instead of scaring him with his own insecurities. Or those of a bully.

"I'll stay away from him." A slow smirk spread across Scott's lips, his finger now tracing a circle around one of Mark's nipples. "You thought I was brave?"

Mark sucked in a deep breath and steadied himself for the pain he was about to inflict on his body. He rolled them over until he was on top of Scott, restraining him with his own weight. "Brave and incredibly sexy. I never thought something like a guy being all macho on my behalf would be so hot."

Scott's smile widened like he'd just learned the best secret of his life.

Mark ran his thumb over those lips, and Scott sucked it into his mouth just like he'd done at the library.

"Soon."

Scott released his thumb. "Is that a promise?"

"You bet." He'd give them both more of what they'd found in the library study room as soon as he could move without wincing.

Too bad he couldn't let go of the image of a panicked Scott crying out in pain.

Even with all they'd talked about, Mark knew what he had to do. What he should've followed through on a long time ago.

This was obviously all new territory for Scott. For both of them, in a way. Mark wanted to take him to places he'd never gone with any man.

* * *

Scott opened the door to Mark's apartment building and stepped into the entryway. He could not believe he was doing this. He was never this forward.

It had been several days since he last saw Mark on the morning after the fight with Bruce. That morning had been awkward as Scott got dressed and said good-bye, and even more awkward when he'd called later that night to check on Mark. They talked for a minute about how long Mark's shift at the library had seemed, and then about the new Dean Koontz novel Scott had finished and which classes he was taking that semester. Nothing about the two of them or seeing each other again. During all of it, Mark had sounded odd, distant. He'd said he had to go but would call the next day.

Since then, they hadn't spoken. Not once.

Lying in that bed talking with Mark had been one of the most intimate moments of Scott's life. Sucked to think that might be all he'd get.

He had to find out if he'd imagined the connection between them. He also had to know if Mark was okay. He lived alone and could've been hurt worse than he'd said. Something could've happened to him. Scott had to check.

But he should've just called.

Too late now. He was at the door to the apartment.

He knocked.

A minute passed. Then another. Finally the door swung open. A stranger stood inside.

He was about Scott's age, taller but with the same build and same blond hair. He wore only a pair of jeans, hanging so low it was clear he'd skipped underwear. His hair was sticking up all over and not in an on-purpose sort of way, more like he hadn't showered since he'd woken up. He wore a thick silver chain around his neck. It had intricate Celtic-style loops engraved all over and was unlike anything Scott had seen before.

The guy leaned against the doorjamb. "You must be Scott."

"Yeah."

"God, you're as cute as he said. Come on in." Almost Naked Guy didn't wait for Scott to move. He turned and went into the living room. He had a sexy swing of his hips that was way too ridiculous to be an unconscious move.

Scott followed him inside.

Almost Naked Guy plopped onto the couch and scanned Scott's body. "I don't suppose you switch?"

Scott halted in the middle of the room. "What?"

The guy waved a hand in the air. "Don't panic. I was just kidding. It's been a long time since I've had several days off in a row, and I'm all anxious. I say stupid things when I get like this." He patted the couch cushion beside him. "Have a seat."

Scott almost asked where he worked, but something about the way the guy had said "days off" had him pretty sure he didn't want to know. Reluctantly, he took a step forward. He glanced at the coffee table before the couch and stopped in his tracks. There was an assortment of ropes, scarves, cuffs, and something metal that looked like a complicated pulley system. Several of the ropes were uncoiled like they'd been used not too long ago. He should leave. Instead he asked, "Is Mark here?"

"Nope." Almost Naked Guy slowly raised his hips and slid a pack of cigarettes out of his pocket. "He had to run to a meeting with his advisor. Something about his dissertation."

"Oh. Okay, thanks." Scott backed toward the door as he spoke.

Almost Naked Guy jumped off the couch. "You can wait for him."

"No, that's okay." Scott kept on going.

"Wait, don't leave. I think Mark might like the idea of the two of us meeting."

That had Scott stopped at the door. He turned. Almost Naked Guy was standing behind him, his thumbs stuck inside the waistband of his jeans like he was about to do a cowboy line dance or shimmy out of the jeans. "I really think he'd like seeing you and me together."

Together? "Whatever. I have to go." Scott spun around and flung open the door.

Almost Naked Guy called after him. "I'll tell him you came by."

Scott waved off the remark. "Forget it." He raced down the stairs and outside.

All Mark had to do was tell him he wasn't interested, that there was someone else, that he didn't want anything exclusive. He didn't have to avoid Scott or make some stupid promise about them being together again. Maybe it had been obvious how much Scott had already been feeling for him. Better to give a guy like that the brush-off than end up with some lovesick stalker.

Scott got the message. He stepped onto the sidewalk and took off in the direction of his apartment. Five minutes later, he was still walking with a quick, aggravated stride. He jumped at the ring of his phone. For a second his hopes rose that it was Mark. Which was stupid. Scott was pretty sure he didn't want to see the guy again.

He checked the display and answered. "Hey, Dad."

"You okay? You sound funny?"

"Yeah. I'm fine. Just walking home."

"You don't sound fine."

Scott sighed. His dad always knew. "It's no big deal. I met a guy and got my hopes up, that's all. I'm okay, really."

"Well, if he wasn't interested in you, then he's not good enough for you."

"Thanks, Dad." He rounded the next corner and headed toward his apartment building. "It's okay. I need to stay focused on the competition and school anyway."

"I like the sound of that."

At least he had his dad convinced.

* * *

Scott slammed the pencil onto the desk and wadded up the paper. He chucked it across his room. The crinkled ball bounced off the opposite wall of his bedroom and landed on his nightstand with the others.

He'd been working on the last page of *The Hawk in the Caverns* for two hours, since he'd gotten back from Mark's. For once the apartment was quiet, but he still couldn't stay focused or get the sketches right. There was something wrong with all six panels. He grabbed the Mountain Dew bottle and chugged the last half. The story revisions were finished. He knew exactly what was happening in the final scene.

Then why couldn't he figure out what he was doing wrong with the art?

Because the judges' comments about the ending kept rolling through his head. They were seriously messing with him.

Or was it something else?

He wadded up the next piece of paper and threw it across the room. "Stupid jerk." He'd meant Mark, but in the silence following his outburst, he was pretty sure he'd actually meant himself.

He dropped his head until his forehead smacked the desk.

It wasn't just the talking or the way Mark had looked at him or the way he'd listened or the way he'd fucked him. It was all of it.

Sitting there with his head on the desk reminded him too much of how Mark had pinned him on that table in the library.

He jerked his head up. He wasn't going to let someone he'd just met make him lose focus. This competition was his shot, and it meant more than some guy. He picked up his pencil and started in on another sheet of paper.

A knock sounded on the apartment door. Probably one of his roommates. They were always leaving for practice without their keys. He headed into the living room and opened the door. Mark stood in the hall. The bruises on his face had faded some. The cut on his lip had healed. He had a backpack slung over his shoulder and wore jeans and a sweatshirt, his hair looking like he, or someone else, had been running his fingers through it all day. Someone probably had. Just not Scott.

Despite his casual appearance, Mark looked tense, anxious. "Can I come in?"

Scott hesitated, a part of him wanting to ask all kinds of questions. Another part wanting to slam the door in his face. "I guess."

Mark stepped inside, his gaze locked on Scott. He held the stare for a moment more, then turned away and set his bag near the door. He went to stand in the middle of the living room, surveying the space.

Scott would've cleaned up had he'd known Mark would ever come to see him. There were empty fast food containers and soda cans scattered throughout the room. On the floor, the end tables, and even a crunched can on the couch beside a pair of tennis shoes with stained gym socks sticking out the top. The room reeked too. Like a team of basketball players had just been there, rubbing their sweat all over the upholstered furniture, which was pretty much what went on there every day.

"My roommates are pigs."

"Jocks?"

"Yeah."

Mark looked surprised. What did he think? A bunch of jocks would never be friends with Scott? True, they'd only asked him to move in and gave him his own room for half price in exchange for help with their coursework, but he wasn't admitting that to Mark. Not now.

"Show me your room."

For a moment Scott considered saying no, but he couldn't let go of the image of Mark in his bed. Even if his heart was warning him to stay clear, his dick sure wanted more.

He gave in and crossed the room. Just because he showed him around didn't mean anything would happen.

Mark followed him down the hall to his bedroom.

This was his space. Small but all his. His twin bed, his dresser, his desk with the wobbly swivel chair that was too small for most people's asses, and his sketch board, the one his dad had bought for him last Christmas. The only thing that wasn't his in the room were the stacks of library books along the back of the desk.

"You should have one of those drawing tables." Mark stepped to the nightstand beside the bed and pointed to the crumpled pieces of paper. "What are these?"

"Garbage. Sketches that didn't work out."

"Can I take a look?"

"If you want, but they aren't any good."

Mark unfolded one. "Aren't any good? This is fantastic. I can't believe you know how to write a story and you can draw like this too." He picked up more scraps of paper. "Why did you throw these out?"

"They're not right."

Mark unfolded another piece of paper. "This is great stuff. The way you show all that emotion on his face and the power in his stance. Is this for a new book?"

"No. I'm reworking the one for the competition."

Mark flashed one of those bright, sexy smiles.

Stupid jerk.

Yep, that time Scott had meant Mark.

"I saw the list of finalists posted at the library today. I had to stop there for my schedule on my way back from a meeting."

Before Scott could say anything, Mark set the papers down and spoke again.

"You should've mentioned you were a finalist last week. We could've celebrated." He moved forward until he stood directly before Scott, watching him intently. "I'm sorry I didn't get in touch with you this weekend. I had something I had to take care of, and it took longer than I expected."

Scott didn't respond. He really wanted to say a few choice words to Mark, but he didn't trust himself not to sound like a jilted lover. They hadn't made any promises to each other. Well, only the ones about more sex and staying away from Bruce Kreger.

Mark continued. "I didn't want to talk to you or see you again until I got a few things straightened out." He studied Scott. "God, I missed you."

"Stop it. Just stop."

Mark's mouth dropped open, but he didn't speak.

Scott crossed his arms over his chest and forced himself to go on. "If you're here for sex, just spell it out. Don't lead me on."

"That's not—"

"I met that guy at your apartment."

"Gage?" The look on Mark's face was pure panic. Yep. Busted. "When? Today?"

Scott nodded, holding his arms tighter to his chest, afraid if he let go he'd show how nervous and disappointed he was.

"He's staying with me for a few days."

"I got that much."

"He's helping me out with something. His boyfriend said he should stay until I had everything I needed."

A laugh burst out of Scott. "From the looks of him, I'd say he probably gave you a lot of what you needed."

"It's not like that." Mark came closer. "I promise you, we're just friends."

Scott turned away and straightened the blank papers on his desk. "Even if that's true, you shouldn't say you'll call and then not call." He really needed to do something about this saying-whatever-was-on-his-mind thing.

"You're right. That wasn't a nice thing to do to someone I'm dating."

"Dating, huh?" He couldn't hold back the sarcastic tone.

He heard Mark step closer. "Did I fuck that up?"

He gave in and faced him. The disappointment in Mark's expression said a lot. Said what Scott really needed to hear right then. No matter what his reason, Mark really hadn't wanted to hurt him. "I don't know."

"I meant everything I said at my place. About us. About wanting to get to know you."

"You don't have to say that. If you're here for sex, you can just tell me the truth."

"I'm not here for sex." He paused, then smirked. "Well, not only sex."

Scott couldn't help but laugh, tension uncoiling in his chest.

"I wouldn't lie to you," Mark added, his tone and expression laced with sincerity. "I'm here because I'm completely captivated by you."

Scott didn't want to be used, didn't want to be the most gullible guy on campus, but he'd always trusted his instincts. He didn't know how to do anything else. "I believe you."

Mark reached out and threaded his fingers through the hair at Scott's nape. "You're the only guy I'm seeing. The only one I'm interested in."

Scott closed his eyes and leaned forward, wanting a kiss to go along with the reassuring words.

"Not yet. Look at me. We need to talk first."

"Okay."

Mark let go of him, took a step away, and tucked his hands behind his back. "Have you ever heard of a safe word?"

All of a sudden swallowing was a chore. "I've, uh, seen some stuff online about it."

"Me too. I never gave it much thought before. I figured since I wasn't getting into anything too heavy, the word *no* was enough."

Scott opened his mouth to speak, but Mark held up a hand.

"Gage is a sub. He was the only one I felt comfortable talking to about this."

Talking about what? Scott wasn't sure he wanted to know.

"I don't know if you saw it," Mark said as he continued, "but that chain around his neck is a collar. He and his boyfriend are into some pretty heavy BDSM. Floggers, whips, collars, slaves, the whole thing. Quite honestly some stuff I never wanted to know about." He paused and considered Scott for a moment. "I've had some questions for a while now. After you and I talked last week, I decided to have a chat with him. He explained a few things."

Swallowing was no longer the only issue. Scott couldn't speak. He liked being held down, liked the warm slap of a hand against his skin when he was turned on, even a rough touch did it for him. But…floggers and whips and pain and humiliation and God knew what else… His stomach churned.

"Gage and I spent some time this weekend talking. He told me a few stories, explained how things in the scene work." Mark was quiet for a moment as he watched him again. "You need a safe word. Something to hold on to when other words might fail you, something so you are in control of everything going on between us, so you are the one who sets the boundaries."

"I…" Scott sucked his bottom lip in between his teeth. All he could think about was a video he'd once seen with a naked man tied to a post, a leather collar around his throat, clamps on his nipples and clothespins pinching his balls, his body whipped until his back and ass and thighs were covered in red stripes. The guy sure seemed to enjoy it, but Scott had known without a doubt it wasn't for him.

Mark scanned his face. "What?"

"I don't want to hurt! I don't want to be hit like that…with a whip or a flogger or anything like that. I don't want to be a slave. Or a dog. Or a pony. I don't want to wear a collar."

A slow grin hit Mark's lips. "That works for me. What we did at the library, at my apartment with the rope and the tie, that was perfect." He paused, and when he spoke again his voice was soft but sure. "I got the impression it was for you too."

"It was." And Scott would give almost anything for more.

"I also think we could take the bondage and control a bit further."

"Yeah, I think so." He'd dreamed of just how far the night before.

"Good. But we both need you to have that safe word."

"Okay." Scott glanced at the closed door to his room. "Now?"

"Yes. So you'll have it whenever you need it."

"Okay. Um…let me think for a minute." He went to his desk and sat. He thought better this way, pencil in hand, a piece of paper before him. Sure enough, he landed on the perfect word. "Volintium."

"The chemical in that superhero Red's blood that gives him his strength?"

Scott dropped the pencil. "You've read *Red Arch-rival*?"

"When I was a teenager." Mark gave a firm nod. "All right. You say *volintium* and we stop whatever we're doing. You can always say no or explain what you want or don't want, but now you have another option if you need it." He moved in closer and reached for Scott. He pulled him out of the chair and wrapped a hand around his wrist. "So you want to keep seeing me?"

"Yes." God, yes.

Mark tightened his hold, not a painful touch, but restraining, arousing. He gripped the other wrist and crossed Scott's arms behind his back, then tugged him closer without letting go until they were touching chest to chest, Scott's arms wound behind his own back.

"You want me again?" Mark asked.

"Y-y-yes."

The confident expression on Mark's face proved he knew Scott's faltering wasn't about being scared or nervous. Scott leaned into the taller man and drew in a deep breath, taking in the scent of the skin at the base of his neck. He let his eyes fall shut as the warmth and arousal washed over him.

Mark gripped his hair and tugged him backward just like he'd done the night they were last together. Mark's mouth covered his, those strong lips and tongue moving over his in long, slow sweeps. No one Scott had ever been with liked kissing this much, or touching or talking or any of the things Mark seemed to like doing with him.

Another kiss, and the intensity built. The press of Mark's lips increased. He gripped the back of Scott's head and deepened the kiss, his tongue moving with more urgency. Then abruptly he pulled back.

"Face the wall."

Scott did, his mind and body relaxing at that firm, strong voice. Any worry about his novel or the contest or anything else faded away.

"Hands up."

He raised his arms and Mark positioned him so his palms were pressed to the wall on either side of his head, his forearms flat against the surface, his chest and cheek and firming cock trapped against the wall. Mark came in close behind him, groin tight against ass, and whispered, "Two nights together, and I'm already addicted to you." He kissed the back of Scott's neck and slid his hands under his shirt, the touch light on Scott's skin as the shirt and Mark's hands rose up his body.

Mark's tongue joined the lips on his neck. There were nips and licks, and Scott shivered, his every nerve ending lighting up.

Mark removed Scott's hands from the wall one at a time, sliding his shirt off without asking him to move, Mark completely in command of his body. He lowered Scott's pants and underwear, and when those were off, forced his legs wider apart. Then he was gone. Scott waited, needing that connection again. Needing Mark's hands, his mouth, his tongue. Something, anything. Just one more touch. He ached for it.

The silence stretched on.

It didn't matter, though. Mark was somewhere behind him. He could feel it.

"Turn around. Arms at your sides, palms flat on the wall."

Mark was standing on the opposite side of the bed, his open hand rubbing his cock through his jeans. Scott waited against the wall, watching that hand move. He trusted Mark to set the pace with the same instinct he'd felt when he took the elevator ride up to the library's seventh floor.

Mark gave another rub of his cock and then approached, rounding the end of the bed in a fluid motion of confidence. "I like seeing you restrained with just my word." He looked at Scott like he wanted to devour him.

That, mixed with what they'd done less than a week ago in his bed—the talking and touching without the sex—had Scott scrambling to hold back his emotions.

Mark stopped before he reached him. "What's the matter?" Then he moved again, taking the last few steps toward him in a quick stride.

Scott shook his head. "Nothing's wrong." Since that first kiss in the elevator, he'd been able to let go, to be in the moment with Mark. He wanted that feeling again. He breathed deep and let himself fall into it. "Absolutely nothing."

"Good. Because I've been dreaming of doing something to you." Mark ran his hands down the front of Scott's bare chest and abs straight to the small dragon tattoo on his hip. He gripped both hips and dropped to his knees. Then his tongue was exploring the dragon. "God, I love this tat." He stroked the hard length of Scott's cock with one hand. "Been dying to suck you."

"Oh God." This was not happening. Scott's entire body shook as Mark's warm breath hit the top of his dick. "What are you doing?"

"Want to feel your cock on my tongue, in my mouth." He held the base of Scott's dick and angled the head toward his mouth. "You are free to move as you'd like. Touch me, touch yourself, fuck my mouth, whatever you need." He leaned forward and licked the tip of Scott's dick.

Fuck, fuck, fuck. Nothing had ever felt like that. Scott hissed as Mark did it again, tonguing all over the head and the sensitive skin below. The wet heat of Mark's saliva covered the end of his cock. Then Mark opened wide and took him deep, sucking his way to the tip again.

"Oh. My. God." How could this feel so different than a handjob? Scott jerked his hips forward and immediately pulled back. Too much. "Wait."

Mark sat back on his heels. "You don't want me to?"

"I...I do. No one's ever..."

"Never?"

Scott couldn't bring himself to say it.

Mark released him and stood. "What the hell kind of men have you been with?"

"Not many." He shrugged. "I usually blow them, or they fuck me, then leave."

"Not this time. This time, I'm sucking you until you come. Unless you don't want—"

"I do!"

And before Scott could dwell on how the squeal of those words must have sounded, Mark dropped to his knees again and had his cock surrounded by that wet heat. Scott's ass hit the wall. He reached out and gripped the top of the desk in one hand and the dresser in the other. He watched Mark's head bob faster and faster. The intensity built with each plunge of his mouth. So different. Real. Powerful. And that was the problem.

Staring down at Mark felt...wrong. He gripped Mark's shoulders. "Please." Mark sucked harder, faster. "Please. Can I..."

Mark sat back in a flash, releasing his hold on Scott's cock. He examined Scott's face, then ran his hands up his thighs. "What do you need?"

Scott reached out and caressed those wet lips that had just been wrapped around his dick. He didn't want this to end but he had to ask. "I want you to, but can I lie down?"

"Absolutely. On your back in the middle of the mattress. I'll be right back. I need to get my bag."

Scott went to the bed. This was better. He didn't even think about his actions. Or wonder what Mark had in mind. He spread out on the bed as instructed.

Mark left the room and was back a moment later. "Move down. Stretch your arms over your head and grab the top of the headboard. Keep your head flat on the mattress." Mark held up two black leather cuffs with buckles, and a length of nylon strap between the two cuffs. He slipped one on Scott's right wrist, tightened it, and looped the strap around one post of the headboard. He ran it along the back to the other end and secured Scott's left wrist, tightening the strap to the perfect length that had Scott's arms spread wide, his wrists pulled tight against the headboard.

Scott loved watching Mark move, watching his muscles tighten and flex as he secured each wrist, his complete concentration on Scott.

When he was finished, Mark asked, "Are you comfortable?"

Scott squirmed, his cock growing harder at the press of the restraints around his wrists. "Yes."

"Good." Mark raised his sweatshirt over his head, followed by a T-shirt, revealing a yellow and purple bruise along his right side. He removed the rest of his clothes, his dick jutting out from his body, thick and ready from just securing Scott. That thought had Scott's own arousal kicking up a notch.

Mark moved to the foot of the bed and stood there, staring down at him. "God, you're beautiful like this."

"Me? You are. I want to touch you. Will you come closer?" Scott tried to lift his arms, and the restraints caught.

"You will not be touching anything. I'll be touching myself, though. And all of you." Mark stroked himself again, this time nothing between his hand and his cock. Scott could see everything. The way Mark's hand squeezed and twisted as he neared the head, the way his hips shifted ever so slightly with each stroke, the way he cupped his balls with his other hand.

Scott held nothing back. Why should he? Mark had said he liked it when a man begged. "Please touch me. Let me suck your dick. Fuck me. Anything." He lifted his arms again, his cock aching, ready to explode. "Please."

Mark finally moved. He crawled up the bed and straddled him, the warm flesh of his ass pressing against Scott's thighs.

God, this felt more than right.

"I'm not going to do any of those things you begged for. I'm going to suck you dry just like I promised, but first…" Mark reached over the edge of the bed for his bag. He sat up and set something cool on Scott's stomach.

It was standing on end, short but thick and flesh-colored. "Is that a plug?"

"It is."

"I've never used one of those."

"I want you to take it for me. Show me how much you'd like to have my dick in your ass the same time as my mouth's on your cock."

"Oh God. I will. It'll be all you."

Mark reached for his bag again. He pulled out a bottle of lube and squirted some on the top of the plug. The lubricant slowly slid down the length. Mark gripped the base and held the plug in place while he spread the lube all over the surface like he was jerking it off. Scott almost couldn't stand watching that hand play with the toy, his own dick neglected, lying against his body. Mark let go of the plug and stood. "Knees up."

The plug shifted on his stomach as Scott lifted his legs until his feet were flat on the bed. Mark retrieved the toy and pressed the tip to his hole.

Scott bore down, groaning as Mark pushed the slick plug inside him. It was smaller than Mark's dick had felt, but there was still that sweet stretch, the desire spiking through him as he took the plug for Mark.

"Nice." Mark shifted the base, pulled the plug in and out just a fraction of an inch but enough that Scott could feel the slide against his sensitive flesh.

Just as he started shifting his hips up and down, Mark stopped.

He bent to his bag again and pulled out a roll of black tape. "This is called bondage tape. It won't stick to your skin, but it will stick to itself and keep you firmly restrained. Legs out straight again. Good. Hold them together."

Starting at his ankles and slowly working up his body, Mark wrapped Scott's legs with the tape, leaving not one inch of his skin bare.

This was unlike anything else. More intense. More restraining. The way it pinned his legs together, the way it forced Mark's hands to move in slow, careful sweeps. Scott was breathing harder and harder as Mark continued up his body, lifting his legs with each pass of the tape, until he stopped it at his upper thighs. He placed a kiss on the dragon tattoo. Then that mouth and tongue worked along Scott's skin toward his cock; wet sucks and kisses continued to his balls, where Mark lingered until Scott was slick all over.

"You ready for me?" Mark asked.

"Yeah. Uh-huh." Scott licked his lips, waiting to feel that suction on his dick again. The plug felt nice but nothing like Mark's touch. His lips, his hands, his every touch had more strength and passion behind it than any toy or fantasy.

Mark straddled Scott's bound lower legs, his weight pinning him to the bed, heightening the anticipation. He slid a hand under Scott's ass and pushed on the end of the plug right as he gripped Scott's cock and lowered his mouth over the length.

Scott whimpered. He couldn't move.

This was nothing like giving himself a handjob. He had no control on the speed, the angle, the suction. Mark did some sort of twist with his mouth at the top, and Scott let out a loud moan. He wanted more of that.

Like always, Mark read his reaction and gave him more.

The pleasure spiked, and Scott's legs shook. His arms pulled on the already tight strap. He couldn't get away from Mark's attention. Nothing felt like that, nothing increased his own desires like knowing that one, simple fact.

Mark's mouth moved faster and faster, and Scott was a goner. He exploded, coming down Mark's throat, and Mark didn't back down, working him through every last spurt to the end.

"Oh God." Scott melted into the mattress.

When Mark released Scott's cock, he sat up and gave it a last stroke, squeezing out one final shudder. He moved to straddle his hips, the brush of bare flesh against flesh reminding Scott how very few times his sexual experiences had involved this much of a physical connection.

Then Mark grasped his own dick. He stared at Scott and jerked himself, every visible, tight muscle of his arms and chest flexing as he grunted and stroked. His hips moved, thrusting his dick into his hand, precum leaking out the tip. He held his gaze locked on Scott's face. "Close."

"Please," Scott said. "I want to see, want to feel it when you come." He shifted his hips side to side as much as he could under Mark. The plug in his ass jostled. He wiggled more and imagined it was Mark inside him, his ass Mark was about to shoot inside.

"Fuck." Mark collapsed forward and took his mouth in a fierce kiss. He thrust hard against Scott's hip again and again.

Scott tried to arch against him, give Mark more to work his cock against, but Scott was tied and taped and he couldn't move. All he could do was take the slamming of body against body. Nothing was more important in that moment than being what Mark needed.

Another hard thrust, and Mark's body went tight. He came, wet heat landing on Scott's skin. He gave several quick jerks of his hips and shot more. "Jesus." Then he stilled, lying over Scott, his warm exhales hitting Scott's shoulder.

A minute passed. Maybe two. Scott wasn't sure how long, and he didn't care. Mark's breathing slowed. He turned his head to the side and kissed Scott's neck. Once. Twice. "That was unreal."

"Uh-huh." Scott sucked in several deep breaths, trying to calm his racing heart. "Thank you."

"It was better lying down?"

"Yes."

"Good." Mark sat up and unfastened the cuffs at Scott's wrists, checking his skin and slowly lowering his limbs to the bed. Then Mark stood and unwound the tape from Scott's legs and gently removed the plug.

When he was finished, he returned and lay beside him. He wiped several strands of sweat-soaked hair off Scott's forehead. "I always want to know what you want, what you need."

"Okay."

Mark wrapped an arm around Scott's waist. He pulled him close and threw a leg over Scott's own. Was it because the bed was too small or because he wanted to keep contact? Mark's next words were unexpected but spoken with such sincerity, it touched something inside Scott that he'd been holding back on since Mark had entered the apartment.

"Thanks for being there for me the other day in the alley. It meant a lot."

"I didn't do anything."

"Sure you did. And I won't forget it." He kissed Scott, a sweet, slow kiss, and Scott couldn't help but wrap his arms around Mark's neck and hold on.

"So," Mark said, "how about a shower? Then pizza and a movie?"

"Yeah. Just as soon as I can walk." Scott hadn't felt this good, this relaxed all week. Then it hit him, as clearly as if he'd spent the last hour thinking about it. He sat up in a rush. "Oh, man. I know what's missing."

Mark rolled to his back and tucked his hands behind his head. "We missed something? 'Cause I thought we did that pretty damn good."

"Not that." Scott lay back. "That...was amazing. I meant my book. The sketches. I know what I need to add." How had he not seen it before?

Mark was smiling at him.

"What's that goofy-ass look for?"

"Hey." Mark nudged him in the side. "It's not nice to call the guy you're dating goofy." He reached for Scott again as if he couldn't stay away, like he had an addiction to his skin. "So when do I get to read this book?"

"Oh." Scott hesitated.

"Unless you don't want me to."

"No. I do. It's just... It's a huge thing to trust someone with."

Mark was staring down at him. "So is your safety. From the moment we met, you've put your life in my hands when you let me tie you up."

"I know. I don't know why I did that at the library. I'd never even talked to you before. Kind of a stupid move." But Scott didn't regret it. Maybe at the end of the semester when they both had to leave town, when they'd have to say good-bye. "I guess... Maybe I'd been..."

"Waiting a long time to get what you needed?"

He met Mark's stare. "Yeah." He paused, then added, "Who knew the library had more than books?"

"You really should get your head out of a book once in a while. There are newspapers and magazines and computers and movies."

"Shut up."

Mark rolled them, dragging Scott on top of him. He reached up and wiped another strand of hair off Scott's forehead. "It's true. If you'd have looked up once in a while I might've approached you sooner. Hell, I should have anyway. Four years ago." He held Scott's gaze for a long moment. Then the sincere expression turned playful. "Just think of all the places we could've had sex by now. In the copy room, scanning your naked ass while we fucked. On top of those long, low shelves in the law stacks. Perfect height for me to stand there stroking myself while I licked your ass and sucked your balls."

"Oh God."

"Straddling my lap in one of the leather chairs in the reference section. Oh, and up against the fiction shelves, your legs wrapped around my hips, and your bare ass pressed against the best sellers."

"Stop." Scott dropped his head to Mark's chest. "You're killing me."

"Nope. I'm prepping you. You're not the only one with an excellent imagination. I happen to have one too. And a key to get in the library after-hours."

Scott couldn't hold back the laugh. Their combined laughter bounced off the walls of his small room, and he felt only slightly foolish as he wished for the time-freezing machine that Red had destroyed in issue #217. Because if he could, he'd make the semester last a hell of a lot longer than four months.

Chapter Five

"What do you mean? It's been canceled?" Mark stared at his advisor across the cramped office space and tried to process what Dr. Wolfe had just said and what it could mean.

His dissertation defense had been postponed. Indefinitely.

Dr. Wolfe didn't say anything for half a minute or so, which felt a hell of a lot longer. The man was always direct, the kind of guy who looked you in the eye and told you the truth about your work, about your potential, whether you wanted to hear it or not. He'd said on many occasions that anything other than sheer honesty only held a person back.

The hesitation wasn't a good sign.

Finally he spoke again. "They need to investigate an allegation before the committee will agree to meet with you."

"An allegation? Against me?"

"I don't know how to say this."

"Just say it. Otherwise I'll think the worst." Mark tried to force a smile but stopped short.

Dr. Wolfe didn't react to the words or the halfhearted smile.

Not good at all.

Instead he turned away, looked at a row of books on the shelves that covered the wall beside his desk. The textbooks and manuals were stacked every which way amid binders and file folders and loose papers. He reached forward and pushed a copy of *Defeating the Modern Tech Criminal* farther onto the shelf so it lined up with the surrounding books.

In all the time Mark had been coming to the office, he'd never seen Dr. Wolfe glance at the shelves, much less touch any of the books. He'd assumed they were more for a show of status than anything else. *Look at everything I know.*

He'd always liked Dr. Wolfe well enough, but those books and the man himself were a reminder to Mark of the kind of teacher he didn't want to become. One who worried more about what he published and who he impressed rather than focusing on the education of his students.

Dr. Wolfe met Mark's stare again. There was pity in that look, and a foreboding Mark didn't want to contemplate. He'd worked too hard for this.

"A student filed a complaint against you with campus security. They've taken it to the local police, who've convinced him to file charges."

"For what?" Did he need to ask?

He should've known Bruce Kreger would never let what happened in that alley go. Should've expected something like this. After all, Mark was the one who threw the first punch.

Dr. Wolfe cleared his throat, splitting the silence between them in the small office. "Sexual assault."

"What?" The shock gave way to more unnerving thoughts. Mark sank back in the chair, letting go of his backpack he'd been clutching since he took the seat in Dr. Wolfe's office and heard the worst news a guy nearing the end of his doctoral program could hear. Well, almost the worst. "Who?"

There was only one person he'd come on to in the past two months. One person he'd made any sort of advances toward. One person he'd fucked.

He shook his head. It couldn't be Scott. Not after the night they'd just shared.

He'd finally taken him out to dinner. The entire experience had been a delight, with that easy way he could just be himself around Scott. He'd gotten the sense that Scott had felt the same. After dinner and the movie—a new superhero action flick—they'd spent that night naked in Mark's bed. It hadn't been all about sex either. They'd talked and kissed and joked around and touched and talked some more. Mark had shared about his senior year of high school when he'd finally accepted he was gay. Scott had told him the story of coming out to his dad. With each moment they'd spent together, with each new conversation, Scott had become more relaxed, more sure of himself.

Maybe that had scared Scott. Maybe their growing connection had. Maybe witnessing that fight with Bruce had rattled him more than he let on.

Maybe Mark had come on too strong.

No, Scott was just as into him. Things had become intense, almost right from the start. That didn't mean Scott couldn't have panicked or freaked out over their conversation about a safe word and the more intense bondage Mark wanted with him.

Mark didn't think he could force the question out again, but Dr. Wolfe hadn't offered any more information. Mark had to know if his gut was right about Scott, or if he'd made a mistake he hadn't even been aware of—like with Dale.

"Who's saying this about me?"

"Actually I'm not supposed to be talking to you about it." Dr. Wolfe paused and sat back in his chair. He let out a long sigh. "It was an undergraduate. A male undergraduate." He stopped again and studied Mark. Dr. Wolfe knew he was gay. Did he actually think he'd done something inappropriate or unwelcomed? "He says you sexually harassed him, then coerced him to do things he wasn't into."

Mark's chest felt tight, the air in the room heavy. A door opened down the hall. The loud shuffle of shoes and conversation burst through the hallway behind him as students exited a classroom. He spotted the paperback novel sticking out the open flap of his backpack. He'd been standing in the hall earlier reading it while Dr. Wolfe finished a phone call.

Mark had found the paperback in Scott's room when he went to pick him up the night before. While Scott had slipped into the bathroom, Mark had spotted the box of books peeking out from under the bed. He'd browsed the collection like Scott had done with his bookshelves when they were first together at his apartment. You could tell a lot about a person by what he read. Especially the books he kept hidden under his bed. The books in the box under Scott's were nothing like the ones he usually checked out from the library.

Mark had felt a little guilty sneaking one into his bag, but with its tattered condition, that book was obviously the most read one in the box. The perfect choice for the inspiration running through his mind. That inspiration won out over the guilt. He'd need the book to plan out the details.

Mentally working through those details had distracted him, had helped him avoid any nervousness about his dissertation defense. So had the man lying beside him in his bed all night.

It couldn't be Scott who'd said this about him.

"Mark."

He looked up at Dr. Wolfe.

"I want you to know I don't for a minute believe this guy. No matter what his reputation is around campus."

Reputation? There weren't many students at a school the size of theirs who had reputations that extended across the vast, diverse campus. Only…the football players.

"It's Bruce Kreger."

Dr. Wolfe hesitated for a moment, then let out a resigned sigh. "That's right. You know him?"

"Yeah. He's lying. He has it in for me."

"I figured it was something like that. He's going about it the right way, then. The university isn't going to take this lightly. Nor the local police. Not after what happened last year."

Yeah. *Well played, Kreger.*

If there was one thing the university administration was deadly serious about, it was any hint of possible danger to their students. The year before, five frat brothers had raped eighteen freshman students over the course of two semesters, using the prospect of instant acceptance and popularity to lure the impressionable, socially ostracized girls to their rooms in the frat house, and using the same pressures to keep them quiet afterward. One of the girls had finally come forward to turn her attackers in at the end of the school year. Only then did the police learn of the others.

The story of such a large number of student sexual assaults had made nearly every national nightly news broadcast. Since then, the university administration planned on never again getting caught not knowing such violence was happening under their noses.

If you wanted to fuck with someone on this campus, it was a smart play. Kreger obviously wasn't as brainless as he appeared.

He also had perfect timing.

Every job offer Mark had received in the past two months depended upon graduating that May, on the completion of his doctorate. If he didn't pass, he'd have to stay for another year, at least.

Who knew what job offers he'd get in a year? Seattle had been his first choice. A place to start over. Far from his old life.

"I've worked my ass off for this."

"I'm sure everything will be cleared up soon," Dr. Wolfe said. "They have to take this seriously and see what happens with the police investigation before they'll reschedule your defense. You and I both know what this boy is saying isn't true. There can't be any way for him to prove it."

Or was Bruce Kreger even smarter than that?

* * *

Mark entered the dining hall and zeroed in on Scott. There weren't many students sitting alone with their heads bent over a book. Almost all the others were banded together in groups, either chatting with wild animation or scarfing down their meals in zest, as if this was their last chance to talk or eat for the rest of the semester.

He approached Scott's table near the floor-to-ceiling windows that lined the walls of the large circular room. Ominous storm clouds were rolling in across the campus, and the dining hall grew darker with every minute. The wind had picked up outside. A storm was definitely on the horizon. Kind of like Mark's life right then.

And there sat Scott, reading and not even noticing the approaching storm.

He had a nearly full plate of food beside his open book, an almost empty bottle of Mountain Dew clutched in his hand. There was a stack of books next to his backpack. All new releases. Someone had spent a few hours at the library. That had Mark smiling, despite what he'd been through since the day before.

"Hey."

Scott's head snapped up. A smile formed. Nothing shy or reserved about the thrill visible on his face at seeing Mark again.

Mark couldn't resist. He leaned down and kissed him.

He'd meant for it to be a quick, publicly acceptable kiss, but Scott's lips lingered over his and Scott wrapped a hand around the back of his neck. A still somewhat tentative grip, yet one Mark didn't want to walk away from.

He needed the touch, the comfort of having Scott close, of being with someone, other than Dr. Wolfe, who would believe him. It sure didn't seem like the cops had.

Would Scott?

Reluctantly Mark pulled away and took a seat across the table. The scent of pizza and garlic bread filled the dining hall. This was the first time he'd felt hungry since the day before. He stole a fry from Scott's plate. It was ice-cold. "How long have you been here?"

"A couple hours. Got started reading and…" Scott shrugged.

Mark gestured to the plate. "You didn't finish your dinner."

"I wasn't that hungry." Scott bounced a little in his seat. "So…what did they say? What questions did they ask? When will you know how it went?"

"Not anytime soon. They had to postpone before we even got started."

"You're kidding. That sucks."

"Not as much as what I spent yesterday and today doing." Mark did not want to admit any of it. Who wanted to date someone with this kind of baggage? The thought of Scott leaving him sent panic surging. An ache worse than any humiliation or frustration during the past twenty-four hours. He wouldn't keep this from Scott, though. Not even if it meant watching him walk out of his life.

Thunder rumbled overhead, and Mark jumped in his seat. He took a steadying breath. "I was taken to the police station for questioning."

Scott's eyes widened. No more bouncy excitement. This sucked worse than the fingerprints and DNA sample, worse than the glare of the cop who'd taken Mark's statement, than the call to a lawyer specializing in this kind of defense.

"Because of Bruce?" Scott asked.

"Yeah, but not for the reason you think." Mark's stomach turned. Either that fry wasn't sitting well or vocalizing the next part to Scott was even harder than the call to the lawyer. "He says I assaulted him. Sexually."

"What?"

He nodded. Not sure he could actually say what Bruce had told campus security and the police he'd done.

"I don't understand." Scott was shaking his head.

"He's trying to fuck with me. I guess he thought this was the best approach. Which is funny when you think about how homophobic he is."

"Yeah. He's risking a lot drawing attention to himself like this."

"The police are investigating the allegations. They want to talk to you. So does the university's Judicial Affairs Office."

"Okay. I'll tell them everything Bruce did."

"Thanks." But what did he do exactly? Besides verbal threats? Mark was the one who'd brought violence into it. "I told them about what happened at the library, that I threw him out and why. I also told them about the fight in the alley, how I'd started it, and what Bruce said about you. My attorney told them my theory that he's just trying to get back at me. I gave them your name and Owen's. I've been cooperating with everything. I guess that's helped. I'm also guessing they don't have any real evidence about the sexual assault, which means so far they're not arresting me."

"Is he saying…you overpowered him?"

Mark laughed. He wasn't a weakling, but anyone could see Bruce had the advantage. "No. He's saying I manipulated him, got him to trust me, then…" He trailed off and let Scott get the gist on his own. "It sounds like all the police know for sure is he and I fought. They have evidence to back that up. He went to the campus police right after the alley. He had my blood on him, my skin under his nails from where he'd scratched me, and a partial fingerprint of mine was on his belt. At first, he wouldn't tell them it was me. I'm guessing he was trying to make it look like he was scared. Then he eventually offered up my name, and they matched the fingerprint and other evidence with the samples I gave them."

"So that doesn't prove the rest."

"So far, no. It's my word against his. But I'll have to go before a campus conduct review board, regardless of what the police do. For the fight alone, I could get suspended. Or worse."

"I can't believe this is happening."

He met Scott's concerned stare. "I'm sorry you're getting dragged into this."

"I'm not. At least you have my word to add to yours." Scott closed the book he'd been reading and slid it into his bag, along with the stack from the library. "I'll go talk to them right now."

"Thank you."

"You don't have to thank me."

"Yeah, I do." Mark stood and smirked, a playful, teasing smile, trying desperately to find the confident voice and demeanor that was part of the thrill of being with Scott. "Saying thanks can be all kinds of fun. After you're done with the cops…"

Scott stared up at him, anticipation building in that wide-eyed gaze.

"Unless you have other plans, I'd like you to come spend the weekend at my place. Help me forget all this for a little while."

Scott leaned forward, the slightest movement that said a lot, at least to Mark. "I'd like that." Scott stood and slung his backpack over his shoulder. "I'm sorry Bruce is doing this to you."

"You didn't even ask me if it was true."

"I don't have to. Even if it wasn't Bruce saying this, I'd know the truth about you."

Relief flooded Mark's chest. "Yeah?"

"Forcing yourself on someone, hurting them like that"—Scott shook his head—"it's not you."

Mark's confidence was returning. "He's not getting away with it. We know he's lying. My advisor knows it too. I've seen Kreger cheating at the library, paying for the answers to exams. In the end, he'll be the one kicked out of school, not me."

"Good because…" Scott glanced around, hesitated; then he slid his hand in Mark's and tugged until they were tucked into the far corner of the dining hall behind the wall of short-term storage lockers. "Because I'm really not ready to say good-bye to you."

"Me neither." Mark kissed him. He wanted to lose himself in Scott, to forget about the questions from the police, the stares as he'd left the station, about what it would mean if he didn't graduate in May.

Avoidance.

Maybe not the best way to deal with what was happening to him, but he couldn't think of one reason why he should walk away from two days and three nights alone with Scott.

But maybe Scott didn't agree. He pulled away, sporting a serious, discouraging frown. "What are we..." His words trailed off.

"What?"

"What are we going to do at the end of the semester? When we have to leave?"

"I really don't know. Let's just focus on right now, and we'll figure the rest out later."

"Okay." The frown hadn't left Scott's face. "Maybe that's not the right move." He stared at Mark's chest as he spoke. "Maybe this will just get harder and harder to walk away from."

"I think you're probably right about that."

"So..." Scott trapped his bottom lip between his teeth.

Mark advanced, backing Scott against the wall beside the lockers, Scott's bag dropping to the floor in the process. Mark grabbed him by the waist and braced his weight against him.

A female student rounded the corner and opened a locker beside them.

Scott's breathing picked up. He licked his lips, kept his arms pressed against the wall at his sides.

The girl finally had her purse and books in hand. Before she turned to leave, she said, "Jeez, you two, get a room."

Mark ignored her and spoke to Scott after she left. "I don't care how hard it is at the end of the semester. I don't want to stop seeing you."

"I don't want that either."

Mark sealed that deal with a hard kiss, all tongue and open mouths pressing together, his fingers tangled in Scott's hair as he tilted his head back.

Scott moaned into the kiss and grabbed on to Mark's biceps.

This was much better than thinking about lawyers or fingerprints or whether Mark would have to walk away from Scott someday. He gripped Scott's wrists and forced them over his head against the wall, giving him a promise of what the night would bring. Scott squirmed under his touch and deepened the kiss. His hunger called to Mark even more than it had when he'd first approached him at the library.

"Let's get out of here."

"Uh-huh," Scott said between rapid breaths, the warm exhales fanning out over Mark's lips.

Mark had to move, had to get them away from such a public place. He released Scott and stepped back.

"If..." Scott swallowed hard. "If I'm staying all weekend, I need to swing by my place, grab some clothes and stuff."

"Sure. But do you really think you'll be wearing clothes this weekend?"

Scott dipped his head, his cheeks turning pink as he picked up his bag and they headed out of the dining hall. "We have to eat."

"We can eat naked. In bed."

That had Scott stopped in his tracks. "I've never done that."

Which gave Mark another fantastic idea. He was playing it around in his mind as they started walking again.

Scott slipped a hand into his, the touch comforting as he held on. Then Scott leaned in and laid his head against Mark's shoulder. "I'm really sorry about your dissertation."

Emotion welled inside Mark. Scott kept on surprising him, kept on showing him that dominance in the bedroom really did lead him to his most enjoyable sexual experiences, but that he also wanted— needed—a partner, a friend, someone who believed in him.

No matter how long he'd been waiting to move away to somewhere like Seattle, finding the perfect blend of both a friend and lover may just be harder to walk away from than he'd ever imagined.

Scott squeezed his hand. "Don't worry. I'll tell them the truth, and they'll see it's Bruce who should be in trouble."

* * *

"Have a seat while I make us something to eat."

Scott nodded in response, but he didn't sit. He was too wound up. He couldn't even concentrate enough to browse more of Mark's books. He paced the living room while Mark pulled containers out of the fridge on the other side of the small apartment.

Scott never would've thought telling the truth would be so hard. He'd known the minute the police officer had started with personal questions about him and Mark that his answers weren't going to help Mark. They were going to do the opposite. Especially when they got to the sex: if Mark liked it rough, if he ever bossed Scott around in the bedroom, if he ever tied him up, hit him, or did anything close like spanking.

Mark came up behind him and wrapped his arms around Scott's chest. "I'm glad you're here."

Scott leaned into the touch, and Mark kissed his neck. Scott dropped his head back to Mark's shoulder and tried to settle his brain enough to fall into the moment, into the feel of Mark's sure hand running back and forth over his chest.

It wasn't working.

He straightened and stepped away. He gestured to a section of the opposite wall that held a series of gold medals hanging from their blue ribbons, all designating Mark the *Most Valuable Player*. "Do you still play?"

"Baseball? I've never played. Those aren't mine." Mark tilted his head to where more awards hung from another section of the wall. "None of these are. Take a closer look."

The medals were dated 1967, '68, and '69, and it wasn't Mark's name on each one.

"They're my dad's. My mom wanted me to take them. I think it hurt her too much to look at them, or maybe she just didn't want to anymore." Mark stared at a trophy perched on a shelf in between a row of books. "He died when I was a kid. An accident at the plant where he worked. My mom...she changed after that."

"I'm sorry." Scott went to him. He reached for Mark's hand and gave it a squeeze, rubbing his thumb over the backs of Mark's fingers. What an ass he'd been. Worried the trophies and medals had meant they were too different to be together. When really, they had more in common than a lot of people their age. Scott may not have ever known his mom, but he'd still felt her loss every day of his youth. He could only imagine what it had been like for Mark.

"Thanks," Mark said with a return squeeze to Scott's hand. "I don't usually talk about it." He met Scott's stare. "With anyone." Despite his words, he continued as he walked to another bookshelf, keeping his back to Scott. "Everything changed after that. Before he died, my mom worked in a bookstore. One of those independent stores with the used books and hard-to-find titles. On weekends, she'd take us with her to estate sales and auctions. Dad would always hunt for old travel guides with people's handwritten notes about their trips. He loved those books, loved talking about all the vacations we'd take once he had enough money saved up."

"Do you have any of them here?"

"No." Mark ran his fingers over the spines of several books on the shelf before him. Mostly children's books. "My mom needed the money. She got rid of most everything she could sell after he died. Except these. And a few others." He touched the books again. "She had given them to me when I was little. I guess she didn't want to take them back. Dad used to read them to me. He loved the ones set in a big city like New York or any foreign country. He'd say someday he'd take me to see every one of those places." Mark finally faced Scott. "But he was stuck in that shitty house, that lousy neighborhood, that even lousier job until the day he died."

Scott went to Mark again. He wrapped his arms around his neck and held on. "I'm sorry you lost him."

Mark wound his arms around Scott, buried his face in his neck. "I was just a kid, but I still miss him. I miss the way my mom used to be."

They stood there locked in the embrace until Scott asked, "Is it just you and her now?"

Mark stepped back. His face had hardened. "No. She remarried when I was in junior high school. He's an unemployed jerk who hates that I'm gay. I've also got three older brothers. They all work in the same plastics factory." He paused. "Where our dad died."

"Are you close with them?"

A laugh surged out of Mark. "No. Thank God." He made eye contact with Scott again. "That sounds awful, right?"

"I don't know. I've never had any brothers or sisters. I don't know what it's like."

"My brothers are miserable people. All three of them. They hate their wives, complain nonstop about their kids, sleep with whatever women they can beg to take them home from the local bar, and they never spend a single day sober." He stared at the books again, the clench of his jaw evident with the slight twitch in his cheek. "I love my mom, but it can be hard to be around them. She thinks my brothers can do no wrong. I knew all through high school I had to get out of there. Had to live somewhere else. LA or Boston or Seattle. I studied my ass off in school so I could have a different life."

Scott tried to push aside how adamant Mark sounded about moving away. "And now you're getting your doctorate."

"God, I hope so."

"You will. Like you said, the only thing Bruce can prove is that fight." He paused, unsure if he should press for more details. Based on the questions at the police station, it had to be bad. "What exactly is he saying you did?"

Mark pulled away and ran a hand through his dark hair, the shake of frustration visible in that one move. "That I've been coming on to him for weeks, until I finally convinced him to meet me in private. That I talked him into letting me tie him up, and then when he begged me to let him go, I wouldn't untie him. Instead I…" Mark sat on the couch, his movements slow, careful, like he'd do anything to avoid saying more, and that scared Scott more than the cop's questions had.

"He said I raped him. Repeatedly. The things he's saying. They're very specific. They're…"

"What?"

"They're some of the same things as what you and I have done. Although, he's saying they were forced on him."

"Oh God. Was he watching us?"

"I don't know. Both this place and your bedroom have windows, but we had the blinds closed. I suppose with the right equipment, or at the right angle, he could've seen through a crack in them."

"That's…"

"Disturbing?"

"Yeah."

Mark looked up at Scott. "I hope it doesn't taint what we've done." Mark had never sounded so unsure, so insecure about their time together. Not even when he'd told Scott about his past boyfriend and how the man had panicked in the ropes.

Scott reached down and ran a hand over Mark's hair, letting his fingers linger in the strands above his ear. "Never. No matter what, it was a private moment. Just between us." Mark laid a hand over his, and that gave Scott the courage to ask the next question. "You're not mad at me?"

Shock filled Mark's eyes. "Not at all. Why would I be?"

"For what I said to that cop. What if they arrest you? Find you guilty?"

Mark grabbed Scott's waist and tugged him down to straddle his lap. "What you and I did was consensual. It's not even related to the shit he's saying about me. They can't just take his word. They have to find some evidence against me."

"The fight—"

"I have to believe my lawyer when he says he'll do all he can to discredit Bruce's statement and prove the fight was nothing more than what it was."

"But the school might still decide to kick you out. What if you can't defend your dissertation? What if you can't get your doctorate? What if you blame me?"

"Wait a minute." He forced Scott to look him in the eyes. "None of this is your fault."

"But you only hit him because of what he was saying about me."

"How is that your fault? That was my doing. And Kreger's. He's the one who's lying. To the school. To the police. He's the one who's spent his years at this university lying and cheating. I'll prove it if I have to." Mark held Scott's face in his hands. He ran his thumbs over his cheeks. That one touch had Scott feeling more important, more cared about than anything they'd done yet.

Mark kept on touching him. "I'm glad you told the truth. I don't ever want you to do anything else."

The relief hit Scott hard and fast. He lunged forward and wrapped his arms around Mark's neck. "I won't let him hurt you."

Mark ran a hand down his back. "You have no idea how much that means to me, but I don't want you near him. He's obviously, completely losing it if he's willing to let everyone think a man raped him."

Scott pulled back. "Yeah, it doesn't make sense. Even if it were true, a guy like him would hide that fact from everyone. Unless he thinks it's the best way to get back at you." Scott shook his head. How stupid could he be? Of course Bruce had been watching them. "Because he knew. He knew my answers to their questions would make it sound like you did the same to me as what he's saying you did to me. I backed up his story."

"It doesn't matter. It's more than that. My lawyer called while you were being questioned. He found out more details from the cops. Bruce was examined when he first made the report to the police. It showed he'd recently had anal sex." He paused. "Rough sex. Very rough. But whoever he'd been with used a condom so there was no physical evidence to tie it to me."

"Then what does that prove?"

"It backs up his claims."

"It doesn't mean someone forced him. Maybe he likes it rough. Maybe that's nothing new for him."

"Could be. In any case, he was either with someone right before our fight or right after."

Scott scrambled off Mark's lap and stood, the rush of adrenaline flowing through him like he'd just downed a two-liter of Mountain Dew. "Maybe we can find out who he was with. Get him to come forward. Get him to admit it if the sex with Bruce was consensual."

"Boy, that would piss off Mr. Homophobic."

"Who cares?"

Mark gripped Scott by the arm and tugged him back down to the couch, this time encouraging him to sit beside him. "I don't want you involved in this any more than necessary. We already know Bruce was fixated on somebody hurting you."

"But..."

"I'll mention something to my lawyer. Maybe he can hire an investigator to find out who Bruce was with." He sat back. His head landed on the back of the couch. "I just want to forget about it for a little while."

And here Scott was going over it again and again. Some boyfriend he was turning out to be. He just couldn't stand the idea of Bruce getting away with his lies and revenge.

Mark lifted his head and smirked. "I have an idea."

That smile and the commanding tone of Mark's voice had Scott relaxing. "I like your ideas." He went to Mark, kissed him, straddled his lap again, pouring all the support and passion into it he could, wanting Mark to really feel it.

When the kiss ended, Mark reached for a drawer in the desk beside the couch. He pulled out a plain brown box. "I want you to go to my bedroom, get naked, and use what you find in this box. Then lie in the middle of the bed on your back, grab the headboard in both hands over your head, and wait for me."

Scott's breathing picked up. A minute ago, he'd been determined to give Mark whatever he needed, to help him forget, if just for a little while, to be there for him and make the moment special.

Now, it felt like Scott was the one getting the special treatment. Without another word or look at Mark, he accepted the box, stood, and hurried down the hall toward the bedroom, his cock growing hard in his jeans at just the thought of finding out what Mark wanted them to do next.

Chapter Six

Mark wanted to take things slowly, to savor the night with Scott, but the idea that Scott was getting himself ready this time made it nearly impossible to keep the desire in check. Mark breathed deep and forced himself to move slowly, no matter how much he longed to see Scott in the items from the box.

He headed across the room to gather the rest of the supplies he needed to go along with the wicked ideas circling his thoughts. Those ideas weren't canceling out the disturbing news from earlier, but they did envelop it in something pleasant and light and…happy.

Which was an odd realization. He hadn't really been what anyone would call happy at any time in his life. At least not since his dad's death.

He'd been focused, driven.

Since he'd met Scott, their time together had been different than any he'd spent with another guy. He'd found more than he'd been looking for, more than he'd thought he wanted with someone.

He covered the tray full of surprises with a towel and headed down the hall toward his bedroom—toward the one person who could help him forget about the past two days.

Although it was more than that.

Mark wanted every moment he could get with Scott. He wanted to explore every delicious thought he'd had since they met. He wanted to get to know everything about him. Every one of Scott's desires and fears and dreams.

Balancing the tray in one hand, Mark entered the bedroom. He nearly lost the tray's contents onto the floor at the sight before him.

Scott lay on the bed as instructed, his hands over his head gripping the headboard. He wore five of the items from the box and nothing else.

"Did I do it right?"

Those whispered words from Scott had Mark's arousal kicking

into high gear. Everything else faded away.

Well, almost everything. He had to take care of one last item. He set the towel-covered tray on the nightstand. Scott glanced at it but said nothing.

Mark tugged a blanket off the end of the bed and hung it from the curtain rod over the lone window, making sure it covered the entire opening. Even with the blinds closed, he wanted something extra in place. Just in case their lying creep was still watching. He faced Scott. "You did it perfectly. *You're* perfect."

That simple way Scott had once again done what he was told sent a thrill of power thundering throughout Mark. He stepped closer to the bed and undressed, never taking his gaze off Scott as he spoke. "God, I love seeing you in my bed like this."

The red fleece-lined leather cuffs around each wrist and ankle looked amazing against Scott's skin. The vision of those four cuffs ready to secure Scott in dozens of ways solidified the two words that kept running through Mark's mind: *he's mine.*

Mark checked each cuff to make sure Scott hadn't secured them too tightly. After examining the last one, he ran his palm over the other item Scott wore—the Superman briefs with the large red and gold *S* emblem on the front. The blue briefs were purposely too small for Scott. They were stretched incredibly tight, accentuating the bulge of his already hard dick. Scott whimpered at the touch, but he never once let go of the headboard.

Now for the sixth item from the box. Mark cupped the front of the underwear, and Scott moaned louder. Mark didn't linger with the touch. Not yet. He tugged the fabric down in the front so he could get a good look at what lay underneath. The red leather strap was taut around Scott's cock and balls. Not too tight but secure enough it would keep Scott hard for longer than usual. Mark slid the underwear back up and over Scott's dick, purposely brushing the sensitive skin under the head of his cock with the fabric. Scott hissed at the contact.

"It's perfect," Mark said. "Did putting it on yourself turn you on?" He brushed his hand over Scott's cloth-covered erection one last time.

Scott's breath hitched. "Yes."

Mark got on the bed and straddled him on all fours. "What's your safe word?"

"Volintium."

"I want you to watch me and don't look anywhere else."

Scott nodded.

Mark settled back on Scott's legs just below the briefs, keeping close enough he could reach the bedside table. And Scott's mouth. He uncovered the tray and reached for the first item. "I know you're into sweet things, but do you like fruit? Watermelon? Grapes? Pineapple?"

"Yes."

"Good. Because you need to eat something."

"I ate."

"You barely touched your dinner and that was hours ago. Were you nervous?"

"Yes."

"About my dissertation defense?"

"Yeah."

He held a piece of watermelon to Scott's lips.

Scott opened his mouth and accepted the bite, never taking his gaze off Mark.

Mark was having a hard time finding the right words. As much as he wanted to be in charge of their sex, he seemed to be the one whose control was slipping away inch by inch. He'd never been in a situation like this. No, not a situation. A relationship like this. He'd never had someone care the way Scott did. Scott gave all of himself to every moment. To have all that attention and compassion directed at him was inspiring...empowering. Mark wanted to be worthy of it. "It means a lot to me that what's important in my life matters to you."

He fed Scott more watermelon, then a few grapes, letting his fingers linger over Scott's moist lips with every bite. He picked up another piece of watermelon and scooted down Scott's body. He squeezed the watermelon in his fist and let the juice drip onto Scott's right nipple.

Scott gasped as the cool fluid hit his chest.

Mark leaned forward and licked up every drop, flicking the nipple with his tongue, adding in a nip with his teeth. Scott squirmed but kept his hold on the headboard. Mark sat up and fed the watermelon to him, watching him lick the juice from his mouth as Mark did the same with what was left on his own lips.

"Tell me about the book you entered in the competition."

With large eyes Scott lay completely still, waiting while Mark reached for more fruit. "The book?"

"Yes, your book."

"Oh...okay... The first-round judges gave all the finalists feedback. I have time to make any changes I want, and then it gets read again by a panel of judges."

"What's it about?" Mark fed him another piece of fruit, this time pineapple.

Scott made a low noise of appreciation at the taste. He licked his lips again and shifted his hips. "It's set in an alternate world. Like ours but with magic and wizards. Where dragons work with the humans to protect their lands from the mountain dwellers. I really love writing from the dragon perspective."

"Hence the tattoo." Mark grabbed another piece of fruit. He painted Scott's lips with the pineapple before feeding it to him. Scott sucked the juice from his lips. Mark's cock started growing harder at the sight. He'd been half-hard since the kisses on the couch in the living room. He slid father down Scott's body and shifted the Superman briefs so he could see the tattoo on Scott's hip. He admired it with the tips of his fingers, then squeezed pineapple over and around it. Bending forward, he sucked the sweet taste from Scott's skin until the juice was gone. Reluctantly he sat up.

Another bite of the pineapple for Scott.

"When did you get the tattoo?"

"A couple of months ago."

"Why then?"

"I found out I was accepted to grad school."

Another bite. "And you wanted to celebrate with something you could see every day."

"Yeah."

Mark bent over Scott's groin again. He slowly, teasingly kissed Scott's cock through the briefs. One wet kiss after another. Then he pulled the waistband down and gave a long lick up the length of his dick. He slid the underwear even lower in the front, making sure they still covered Scott's ass. He sat back and admired the view of his cock and balls lying outside the blue briefs, the waistband of the underwear tucked under the cock ring.

"Look at you." His superhero. In more ways than one. "Tell me more about your book. About the dragons."

Scott's breath hitched again as Mark went back to wetting his cock.

"They live... I can't...I can't think when you're doing that."

"Too bad. You've had something to eat. Now it's my turn." Mark reached for another piece of the pineapple and squeezed more juice onto Scott's body. This time over his cock and balls. Scott's breathing picked up, but he still didn't let go of the headboard.

Mark ran his lips over and around the head of Scott's dick, then took him in deep, sucking hard until he reached the head again, taking in the taste of the fruit and of Scott. He repeated the action, letting Scott's cock slide along the inside of his cheek this time. He released him. "Keep talking."

Scott moaned again as Mark gave his dick more attention. He alternated between shallow and deeper sucks, trying to keep Scott guessing on what he'd give him next.

Finally Scott spoke. "The dragons live in a three-mile-long cavern. A force of—" He arched off the bed. "Oh God, that feels so good."

"A force of what?"

This time Scott raced through his words. "A force of the mountain dwellers lead an army into the caverns to exterminate the dragons. A group of volunteers made up of local farmers and craftspeople try to help the dragons, try to protect them. The caverns are based on the Ohio—Oh God!" He surged his hips off the bed, filling Mark's mouth with his cock.

Mark lifted his head. Scott kept surprising him. "Based on the Ohio Valley Caverns?"

"Yeah."

"No kidding? I love going there. I can remember the first time my dad took me."

"Oh man!" Scott raised his head and removed his right hand from the headboard, excitement radiating off him. "You've seen them?" He stilled. "Sorry." He put his hand back. "They are supposed to be awesome. They have one of the largest known underground rooms."

"You've never been there?"

"No. I just did a bunch of research."

"But it's only a two-hour drive from here."

"I know, but I didn't have a way to get there."

"We'll have to go sometime. I'd love to show you."

Scott's eyes widened again. "Really?"

"Definitely." Mark moved up Scott's body. He wiped the juice from his own hands using the moist towel he'd brought with the other items. He peeled the banana next. He took a bite, then asked Scott, "You like bananas?"

"Uh-huh. I used to practice with them." Scott's cheeks pinked, but he kept his gaze on Mark as he'd been told to do. "You know, before I could buy stuff online."

"Practice?"

"Sucking someone off."

"Damn." Didn't that create a great mental image? Mark held the banana to Scott's mouth.

Scott didn't just take a bite. He lifted his head off the bed and drew the entire length of the banana into his mouth like Mark had done with Scott's cock just moments ago. Scott bobbed his head, sucking and wetting the banana between his lips. A couple more long sucks, and he pulled back. Which was good. As much as watching Scott's "practicing" mesmerized Mark, he didn't want him to choke on a wet, mashed banana.

Scott licked around the tip of the banana, smirked, then chomped off a huge bite.

"Hey! Don't you dare ever do that to my dick."

Scott laughed as he chewed. No, more like giggled. That infectious laughter eased the remaining tension in Mark's mind and body.

Scott swallowed the mouthful and grew serious. His brows drew in, his expression thoughtful. "I would never hurt you."

"I know that."

They weren't really talking anymore about Scott potentially biting off the end of Mark's dick, or about physical pain at all.

Mark said, "I'd never hurt you either."

Scott nodded. He opened his mouth, then stopped short of speaking and bit his bottom lip like he wanted to say something but wasn't sure how or maybe even if he should.

Mark held his breath, waited, fairly sure he should be doing something to stop the words before Scott could say them but not really wanting to.

Scott closed his eyes and said nothing, his breathing uneven, his fingers twitching from where they held on to the headboard. He was scared.

"Hey."

Scott opened his eyes.

Mark offered him a smile. Time to give them both something else to focus on. He slid off Scott and said, "Let go of the headboard and turn over." Now that Scott had eaten, it was time to use the cuffs.

With something that seemed like relief mixed with anticipation, Scott flipped over in a flash.

"On your knees, head down, hands along your sides."

Mark got off the bed and secured Scott's wrists to the D-rings on the ankle cuffs so his ass was in the air, his head pressed to the bed, his dick still stuck out the top of the briefs, hanging low toward the bed but not touching the mattress. Mark ran a hand over the ass covered in blue fabric. "Beautiful." Not just the way Scott looked— bound, his ass in the air, ready for Mark to fuck him. It was also the way Scott had moved with Mark's words. No doubt or worry or hesitation in his actions. Mark breathed deep, willing his body to hold back before this was all over too quickly. He slapped Scott's ass, and Scott whimpered. His breathing came in harder and harder pants.

Mark got on the bed again and moved in close, kneeling between

Scott's spread legs. "I have a confession to make." He tugged on the underwear, raising Scott's ass higher into the air.

Scott groaned at the manhandling.

Someone liked that.

Mark smacked his ass again. "I took something from your room the other day. You had so many I didn't think you'd miss just one."

Another few deep breaths, and Scott finally spoke, his voice tight. The spanking was really getting to him. "What…what was it?"

"They were in a box under your bed. Like maybe you didn't want anyone to see them." Mark draped his body over Scott's and whispered in his ear. "Paperback novels. Gay romances. Pretty erotic ones too."

OH GOD. SCOTT pressed his forehead into the mattress and wished he could disappear.

No, not really. No matter how embarrassed he was, he didn't want to miss a minute with Mark.

Mark reached over Scott's shoulder to the tray on the table. He uncovered something else and pulled the tray forward so Scott could see the book.

One of his favorites.

"This is pretty hot stuff," Mark said. "And romantic."

"You read it?"

"Oh yeah." Mark sat up. He stayed close, but they no longer touched. "I take it from the condition of this one, you've read it more than once."

"Yes." Scott shifted his head and tugged at the restraints. He couldn't stop himself. He wanted—needed—to feel Mark, to feel their bodies pressed together again.

"Are you uncomfortable? In pain?"

"No."

"Embarrassed?"

"Yes."

Mark smacked Scott's ass again.

That sharp sting, even through the underwear, felt incredible. Like he was flying, a rush of need flowing out from his middle to every part of him, to the ends of his fingers and toes, to his tightly wrapped balls.

"Don't be embarrassed. It's a fucking hot book. Nothing to be ashamed about." Mark spanked him again. "I want to know everything about you. All your secrets." Another swat. "Don't keep them from me."

"I won't. I promise." Scott squirmed, trying to get closer to Mark, wanting another smack on his ass. "More. Please."

Mark gave him more. Three quick slaps. Then he bent over Scott, pressing his groin to Scott's now warm ass, and asked, "Are you turned on picturing me reading it?"

"Yes."

"I jerked off to it," Mark added.

Oh God.

"Did you?" Mark asked.

"Yes."

"You like reading about three men in bed together?"

"Yes."

Mark wrapped an arm around Scott's chest, supporting his weight. He gripped him by the hair and tugged his head up.

That one forceful move always did Scott in. He held back on the desperate need to come. He didn't want to lose it yet, didn't know if he even could with the strap around his balls.

Mark tugged again. "Don't get any ideas. We are not having a threesome."

"No!" Scott squirmed, trying to look back at Mark.

"Be still. You're going to hurt yourself." Mark let go of his hair and lowered him to the bed.

Scott tugged on the restraints again and again. "I don't want anyone else. It's just a book."

"Take it easy." Mark ran a hand down Scott's back. "It's okay."

"It's just... I thought it was..."

"What?"

"Beautiful. How they all love each other."

Mark kept rubbing Scott's back. "Yes, it was." That hand was gone and another smack landed on his ass. "I think," Mark said, "this is one of my favorite parts." He reached for the book and laid it on Scott's lower back, holding it in place with one hand. He started reading. "*I got on my knees behind him and stroked the taut curve of his ass. I liked the look of his pale skin under my hands, the feel of his heated flesh. The sight of him bent over in front of me had me ready to go off. The skin of my dick stretched tight.*"

Scott wanted to shout at Mark to stop reading. That strong voice saying such intimate, delicious things had Scott's desire burning through him. "Please."

Mark went for the tray again. Scott spotted the lube and condom as Mark grabbed them. Then Mark wrenched sideways on the Superman briefs until they covered only half of Scott's ass. He kept reading.

"Richard handed me a condom. My hands trembled as I opened the rubber and slipped it on my dick. I added lube, and my balls drew up from my own touch. I wasn't supposed to need someone that much. I wasn't supposed to be out of control. I leaned over Matthew and licked and nipped the back of his neck, savoring his taste, his scent— my brain already equating that smell with physical pleasure and sated bliss. The responding moans and sways of his body would have made anyone think I'd already entered him. He needed me as much as I did him. I lined up, the head of my dick pressing at his opening. 'Hold there,' Richard said. His deep voice cut through the surge of desire, and I stilled. He forced my legs apart. His cock slammed inside me with a fast thrust that drove my body forward into Matthew."

And with those words Mark pushed into Scott.

Fuck. Fuck. Fuck. Scott bit his lower lip to keep from crying out at the intense pleasure that shot through him. Mark had neighbors, after all. Scott fisted the sheet at his sides in both hands. His arms locked in place, he couldn't move, couldn't do anything. Could only accept every shove of Mark's dick into him, the slam of their bodies coming together. The book slid off his back and landed beside him.

Mark leaned over him and spoke in his ear, using the strong, commanding tone Scott had loved from the start, each word accentuated with a thrust into him. "You…are…mine."

"Yes! Yes, please."

Mark kept moving. With one hand he unfastened the cock ring from around Scott's balls and reached for the lube. Then his moist hand stroked Scott's cock, nothing slow or easy, a quick jerk like he was on a mission to get Scott to come harder than ever.

Scott wanted to hold out, let Mark come first, but he'd lost complete control of his body. He came, every part of him shaking. He tried to throw his arms out. The restraints caught, and his legs spread wider. Mark groaned as he continued pushing into him.

"Almost. Just…" Another thrust, and Mark's body stilled. Then his hips jerked several more quick snaps as he came inside Scott, groaning and grunting louder than Scott had heard from him before.

The room grew quiet in the aftermath of their heavy pants. Mark stayed buried inside him for a minute. Then he cupped Scott's ass cheeks as he pulled out.

A few seconds later, he repositioned the underwear more comfortably in place, unfastened Scott, and removed the cuffs. He lowered him to the bed and lay beside him, wrapping a leg over both of Scott's, holding him close. "I want to read *your* book next. The one from the competition."

"Oh, okay." Scott was too sated to give much thought to the idea that Mark really would be reading his book soon.

Mark held him against his chest, tucking Scott's head under his chin. Scott was still sticky all down his front from the fruit.

"You want to go take a shower?" Mark asked.

Scott did, but not more than he wanted this moment. "In a minute."

They were quiet for a while, the embrace saying more than words—or at least more than any words Scott could come up with right then.

"Thank you," Mark whispered, his hand slowly running down Scott's back, over his ass, and back up again.

Scott lifted his head and studied Mark—the usually confident man who now wouldn't meet his stare. "What for?"

"For giving me what I needed. For knowing what that was even more than I did."

Scott laughed. He had started the kissing on the couch with every intention of helping Mark forget what was going on with Bruce. Then the entire moment had somehow transformed into something else. Scott had merely been reacting with honesty to everything. "You're welcome, but I think we just got really lucky here."

Mark brushed several strands of hair off Scott's forehead. "Yeah, we did."

Scott settled back in Mark's arms, confident that Mark got what he'd meant.

* * *

Scott stared at the piece of paper in his hands with the address he'd written down earlier that day, more unsure of what to do than ever. But hadn't he looked up the address for a reason? He knew what he wanted to do—what he needed to do. It was all he could think about since he'd gotten home from Mark's that morning before his first class.

Someone snapped his fingers before Scott's eyes. "You awake in there?"

"Huh?" Scott looked up.

Owen stood beside his table at Not Just Java. "You look like you're thinking too hard. Worried about the contest?"

"Nah. Just got a few things on my mind today."

"Well, I'm just about to close up for the night, so you'll have to save your thinking for tomorrow."

"Right." Scott stood and started collecting his books and his latest sketches for *The Hawk in the Caverns*.

Owen laughed. "No hurry. Take your time." He set to wiping the surface of a nearby table, and without looking Scott's way he asked, "He's good to you?"

Scott stilled, his sketchpad in his hand. "What?"

"I only need one guess who you were a million miles away with."

Scott never could hide what he was feeling from most people who bothered to look. "Yeah, he's real good to me."

"Then why all the worry?"

Scott shrugged. He tucked the sketchpad into his bag and caught sight of the red marks and light bruises circling his left wrist. Both wrists actually had marks on them. He'd always bruised easily, and he'd wiggled so much he'd pulled the cuffs to the point of leaving the marks. His wrists didn't hurt. In fact, he loved the reminder of what they'd done.

The weekend at Mark's hadn't been *all* about sex. They'd hung out in bed most of the day on Saturday, watching a couple of Mark's favorite movies on his laptop and exchanging blowjobs in between. On Sunday Scott sprawled out on the ugly plaid sofa in the living room and read while Mark worked on a computer he was fixing for a coworker. Then on Sunday night, they'd managed a repeat performance with the wrist and ankle cuffs.

Scott tugged the sleeves of his sweatshirt down, afraid Owen would misunderstand if he saw the marks, especially after the fight he'd witnessed in the alley between Mark and Bruce. Scott didn't want to have to explain how much he enjoyed everything he and Mark did together. He wasn't sure who he'd embarrass more, him or Owen. He smirked at that as he zipped up his bag.

"Well, then, I hope whatever's got you so distracted from your books and drawings isn't about that guy."

"Mark?"

"No. That football player. I don't trust that kid."

Yet another reason for Scott to like Owen.

"He's trying to get Mark into trouble."

"About the fight?"

"No. Something much more serious."

"Anything I can do to help?"

"I don't think so." But there was something Scott could do. He slid his backpack on. "Thanks, Owen. I gotta get going."

"See ya tomorrow?"

"Yeah." That's if he wasn't arrested for stalking a football star before then.

* * *

Scott had never been in this part of town before. There were no streetlamps, no houses with their front porch lights on illuminating the way for pedestrians. In fact, there were no other pedestrians at all. Only Scott. And Bruce.

Following Bruce to learn what he was doing, where he went, and who he might be seeing had seemed like a good idea earlier that day when Scott had looked up Bruce's address. Now that it was dark and raining steadily, and now that he'd been following Bruce on foot for twenty minutes across town, Scott wasn't so sure. He was cold and wet. Thank God his backpack wasn't the cheap cloth kind. His books and drawings were probably safe.

At this rate he was beginning to think Bruce wasn't really headed anywhere. Maybe this was how he got in his nightly exercise.

Then Bruce stopped, and Scott did the same, keeping to the safe distance he'd been trailing behind him with since he saw Bruce leave his apartment.

Bruce hesitated, then walked up to a single-story gray house covered in peeling paint. The place looked more run-down than the cheap college rentals near campus that were used more for partying than sleeping. Bruce knocked on the front door and waited.

Scott crept forward, hoping to hear why Bruce was there. He hid behind a tree near the curb, probably not close enough to hear anything, not with the heavy rainfall all around him, but he did get a good look at the bald man who answered the door.

He wore a black Harley-Davidson T-shirt depicting a bike jumping through a ring of flames. The sleeves were cut off at the shoulders, tattoos covering both of his arms. He gave a nod, brushed past Bruce, and headed into the rain. Bruce followed, his gaze locked on his own footsteps while the two marched along the dirt driveway toward the back of the property.

They went behind a smaller building, a garage not connected to the house. Scott crept forward again, this time in the grass along the driveway, carefully avoiding the puddles as not to make any noise, even with the heavy beat of the rain. By the time he neared the small garage at the end of the drive, his shoes were caked with mud. He made his way alongside the building. When he reached the back, he peeked around the corner. The two men stood between the building and a tall wooden fence that blocked them from being seen by any of the nearby houses. A tarp hung like a canopy from the roof of the garage to several fence posts, protecting the bald man and Bruce from the onslaught of rain.

Scott hunched down behind three metal garbage cans at the corner of the garage and watched the two men who were illuminated by a lone light that seeped over the top of the fence, probably from a window of the house in the lot behind them.

The bald man leaned against the exterior wall of the garage. Without a word, he tugged Bruce forward by the back of his neck. There was no kissing, no embrace, just the bald man's hand grabbing one of Bruce's and forcing him to rub his dick through his jeans.

After a few strokes, the guy tore open his pants. "On your knees, asshole." He shoved Bruce to his knees, and Bruce landed hard in the mud, drops splattering all the way up onto his face. That didn't seem to faze him. He took the other man's dick in his mouth and swallowed him down to the base. No gagging or shocked reaction.

Bruce Kreger had definitely sucked cock before.

A hand landed on Scott's shoulder. He spun around, almost smacking his arm into one of the metal garbage cans. Mark was behind him, also soaking wet and looking pissed—more than when he'd been fighting with Bruce in the alley. He gestured for Scott to come with him away from the garage.

Scott shook his head and tried to encourage Mark to look around the corner of the building, but Mark didn't move. Then low grunts came from behind the garbage cans, louder than the rain hitting all around them. Mark's angered expression grew curious. He crouched beside Scott and peered around the cans, then glanced back at Scott, eyes wide. Mark fumbled for his phone, shielding it from the rain, a feeble attempt at best. He snapped a couple of pictures and quickly tucked the phone away, then gestured with a tilt of his head toward the street.

"But…" Scott whispered. He motioned toward Bruce and the bald man.

Mark mouthed the word *no* and jerked his head toward the street again, a defiant look on his face.

Scott turned away, not wanting to see that look from Mark any longer. He made his way down the driveway toward the street and waited on the sidewalk. Mark approached in a quick stride, grabbed Scott's arm, then got them moving again. When they were a few houses away, Scott spoke, nearly shouting in order to be heard over the continual roar of the rain. He had to know what Mark was thinking.

"We need to talk to that guy. Maybe he was who Bruce was with after the fight."

Mark said nothing. He kept walking, never slowing the agitated strides, his jaw tight, his expression one of frustration. Was he angry with Bruce? Or Scott?

Scott had to hurry to keep up with him. "Mark…"

Nothing.

The rain was coming down harder, but there was no way Mark could've missed Scott's plea. Or the concern in his voice.

Scott gripped Mark's arm, forced him to stop. "Talk to me."

Mark looked more than just angry now. Confused, maybe. Conflicted. "I can't believe you followed Bruce here. After I told you I didn't want you involved."

"But…I am involved. I'm involved with you. What affects—" What was he doing? Scott didn't like the idea of holding back on what he felt, what he knew to be true, but he also had this unease running through him about saying too much too fast, especially right then.

Mark searched Scott's face but said nothing. Finally he sighed. The anger faded as he tilted his head toward the sky. Raindrops splattered onto his face and ran down his cheeks. He met Scott's stare, and Mark's facial features lightened like he'd made up his mind about something or had come to a realization. "Let's go. We have to get out of here before Bruce sees us." He started walking, and Scott followed.

Without saying anything more, Mark headed in the direction of Scott's apartment.

* * *

Mark stopped behind Scott at the apartment door, but Scott didn't enter. Mark waited, saying nothing, listening to the water drip from their drenched clothes to the hallway floor, staring at the back of Scott's head. The blond hair was much darker soaking wet. Neither of them had said a word since their brief exchange in the rain, which had Mark feeling like the biggest asshole. Scott had only been trying to help.

Mark wanted to get them inside and forget the entire night, but he didn't want to tell Scott what to do. Not right then. Mark was still upset. He needed to explain rationally why Scott had to stay away from Bruce. Not talk to him with anger or condemnation, or tell him how to live his life. He wanted Scott to understand him, to listen to him, not fear him.

Never that.

Behind the apartment door came the sounds of explosions from a movie or video game. Then the resulting cheers from whoever was inside poured out through the closed door into the hallway.

Scott didn't move, but he finally spoke. "My roommates are in the living room." He held still, his back to Mark. "We need to talk, and I don't want to do that here, with them around."

"We're just here to pick up some of your stuff. You're staying with me until this is all over." So much for keeping quiet and not telling Scott what to do.

Until this is all over? Was he talking about the thing with Bruce? Or whatever was happening between them? Mark wasn't sure. "Apparently you need someone around to make sure you don't get into trouble."

Scott whirled to face him. "I can take care of myself. I don't need you telling me what to do."

That had Mark silent again.

Scott looked like he regretted his words or maybe the angered tone with which he'd spat them at Mark.

"I know that." Mark reached up and cupped Scott's cheek. With his thumb, he wiped away a drop of water that had dripped from Scott's hair to his face. "I don't want to boss you around." He tried for a smirk. "Outside the bedroom, that is. I just... I need you to be careful. I don't want this thing with Bruce to touch you any more than it already has."

"You can't stop that. What affects you affects me."

Mark closed his eyes and leaned in, pressing their foreheads together. "That's why I can't let anything I've done or said—" He stopped himself and pulled back.

"You forget," Scott said, "the whole reason Bruce and you got into that fight was because of what he said about *me*, because I sat in *his* chair at the library. He's the bully who started all this."

More explosions and hollers from inside the apartment erupted through the door.

Scott reached for the doorknob. "Just ignore them, okay?" He opened the door and moved quickly across the living room toward the hall leading to his bedroom.

One of the guys sitting on the couch holding a game controller called after Scott. "Hey, kid, I've got a soc exam next week. You gotta help me figure out what's gonna be on the test."

Scott paused before heading down the hall. "I will. Meet me at the library after your last class on Wednesday."

"Thanks, man."

"No problem." Scott got moving for his room again.

None of the other three roommates said a word, acknowledged Mark, or even looked up from the game. Mark followed Scott. His frustration grew with each step. This time aimed more at the stupid-ass roommates who were using Scott.

In the bedroom Scott had a duffel bag open on the bed and was tucking clothes inside, his every move erratic and agitated. Not a reaction Mark had seen from him before.

Mark closed the bedroom door and waited silently by it, feeling unsure and not liking the insecurity of that at all.

Scott shoved several pairs of socks into his bag. He paused, staring down at the open bag. "Why didn't you want to talk to that guy with Bruce?"

"I didn't want Bruce to see us there. I know where that bald guy lives. I can go back to talk to him."

"You followed Bruce there?" Scott asked.

"Yeah. From his place."

"I didn't see you."

"I kept to the other side of the street. After he went out behind the house, I spotted you heading down the driveway."

Scott shrugged. Other than that, he hadn't moved. He still stared at the duffel bag. "Guess I'm not very stealthy."

"You did pretty good. I didn't see you until then."

This was not how Mark wanted this conversation to go. He reached for the doorknob behind him, needing to hold on to something. "You really shouldn't have gone there." He tightened his hold on the door. "I don't want anything to happen to you. I don't want him to say anything about you. Or worse. I couldn't stand it if—"

Scott faced him. One look at Mark, and he came to him. "I had to do something." He ran his hands down Mark's arms, a soothing touch, gentle and so very different from the frustration he seemed to have been packing his bag with. "Please don't be angry with me." He took a hold of the hand Mark had plastered around the doorknob and encouraged him to let go. "You would've done the same for me." He leaned in and kissed Mark. So sensual, the way Scott touched him, comforted, taking charge of the moment and turning it into something else.

Who the hell was the dominant one in this relationship?

Mark knew the answer as soon as he thought the question. Their sexual play had nothing to do with who was stronger or more certain of what to say or do in any moment. Mark's entire body relaxed. "You're right. I would've done whatever you needed me to."

Scott nodded. He went to the bed and sat beside his bag. "What should we do now?"

"I'm going to confront Bruce tomorrow."

"Shouldn't you talk to the police? Or your lawyer? Those pictures on your phone don't prove anything. Other than he was embarrassed to admit he's gay. It doesn't change what he's told them, the evidence they have."

"I've got to get him to tell them the truth. And if he doesn't...he'll get to see those pictures all over the Internet."

Scott stared at him with a stunned expression.

"You don't like that plan?"

"I just think... It's like we're sinking to his level. Maybe we should just talk to him. Not threaten him. Maybe we can get him to see how ridiculous all this is. If he takes this any further, so many people are going to be furious with him for wasting their time."

"A guy like him is not going to back down because you ask him nicely."

Scott didn't say anything to that.

"What are you thinking?"

"Nothing. You're probably right." He stood and came to Mark. "I'll be right back. I've gotta grab my toothbrush and stuff from the bathroom."

Mark hesitated where he stood blocking the bedroom door. "You okay with staying at my place for longer than a weekend?" He had to ask. As much as he wanted to keep Scott safe, he needed this to be Scott's call.

"Yeah. I just wish..."

"What?"

Scott shook his head. "Nothing."

"Stop that. Tell me. You wish what?"

"You had asked me to stay for a different reason."

Mark stepped closer, unable to keep from touching Scott when he said something like that. He wrapped his arms around him and pulled Scott against his chest. "I *asked* you to stay because I'm worried about you. I'm *glad* you're staying because I really do want you there. I want us to be together as much as we can before..."

Before what? He was arrested? The end of the semester?

Scott didn't ask for clarification. He offered a smile and a nod and headed into the hall.

IN THE BATHROOM Scott pulled out his phone and dialed. He sat on the edge of the bathtub and tried to focus on the ring of the phone. Not on the man waiting in his bedroom. When his dad answered, Scott kept his voice low while trying his best to sound normal at the same time.

"Hi, Dad. What are you doing?"

"Hey, kiddo. Nothing much. How's everything going?"

"School's good. Sent you some links from my Ancient Greece class I thought you'd like to check out."

"I got those, thanks. Very interesting stuff." When Scott didn't say anything else, his dad's voice changed to a more serious tone. "So what's up?"

Scott never could hide anything from him. "There's something I wanted to tell you." He couldn't stand to keep this from his dad any longer. He wished he could do this in person, wished his dad was closer so he could actually meet Mark.

"Okay. What is it?"

"I'm seeing someone."

"The same someone you said it didn't work out with?"

"Yeah. Turns out I misunderstood something. We're gonna be spending some more time together." He paused. "Dad, I really like him."

"That's a good thing."

"Yeah."

"Then why do you sound so scared?"

Scott eyed the closed door of the bathroom. "This is really intense."

His dad chuckled. "The best loves usually are."

"He's moving away after graduation."

The sigh from his dad came across the line loud and clear. "This may not be what you want to hear, but you can't always worry about tomorrow. I knew your mom for three years before we got married. You were born a year later. That means I only had four years with her. Not long in the grand scheme of my life, but I would never take them back or do anything differently, even if I could erase the pain. That's what real love is like. Sometimes you just gotta embrace the good things in life and see where they take you."

"Okay. I get what you're saying."

"Scott?"

"Yeah?"

"Where are you?"

"In the bathroom."

"Is he there in your apartment?"

"Yes."

"Hang up the phone, get out of the bathroom, and live."

"Okay. Thanks, Dad."

"Be careful, please."

"I will."

"Condoms."

"Dad!"

"Promise me."

"I promise."

His dad laughed, said good-bye, then hung up.

Scott stared at the phone in his hand. Maybe if he didn't think about Bruce's accusations or graduation or Mark moving away, then everything would just fall into place.

Or maybe not. Maybe this was all they'd ever have.

His dad was right. Some things were too good not to go for, no matter how they turned out in the end, no matter how much a part of him still wanted to believe he'd get a happy ending, just like all those romance novels hidden under his bed.

He returned to the bedroom, tossed his toothbrush and shaving kit into his bag.

Mark was sitting at the foot of the bed staring out the lone window of Scott's room.

"Ready to go?"

Mark didn't respond or move.

"Mark?"

"Maybe we shouldn't do this."

"What? Go to your place?"

"Maybe you shouldn't stay with me. I was angry with you."

Scott went to stand in front of him. "That's okay. You were worried. All couples fight sometimes."

"But...the other night at my place... What we did with the cuffs and the spanking... I don't want to be together like that when I feel this way."

As naive and silly as Scott usually felt when it came to men, it surprised him how inexperienced Mark sounded.

Scott sat beside him. "Every single night we're together doesn't have to be like that. That's way too much pressure—on both of us." He paused, knowing he had to say the rest but wanting to get the words right. "Being with you has become about much more than the sex for me."

Mark slowly looked Scott's way, his dark eyes more at ease and certain. "Me too."

Chapter Seven

Mark awoke to the oddest sensation. He could feel the heat of Scott's body beside him. He opened his eyes and found the bedroom still dark. The rain pounding against the window as the storm continued its onslaught added to his feeling of unease. His eyes adjusted to the darkness.

Scott was leaning over him, watching him. "Are you awake?"

Mark laughed. "I am now."

A loud crack of thunder ripped through the room, startling him. So did the look of worry on Scott's face that was visible as another flash of lightning lit up the room. Mark scrambled for the lamp on the bedside table. "What's wrong?"

"I want to go with you when you confront Bruce."

"What?" Mark moved to a sitting position. "No way." He tried for a calmer tone. "I don't think that's a good idea."

Scott pulled his legs up under him so he sat on the bed facing Mark. The plaid flannel pajama pants and white long-sleeve cotton shirt he wore had him looking much younger than usual. They'd both been frozen when they got to Mark's after their stroll through the rain. Mark had forgone his usual insistence that Scott strip down to nothing, and they'd dressed for bed. Although Mark had skipped a shirt with his sweatpants. He'd been glad about that as soon as Scott had settled into the bed with his head on Mark's chest. That was the last thing he remembered before he drifted off to sleep.

What time was it? Had Scott gotten any sleep?

"I don't think..." Scott breathed deep, as if summoning the courage to say more. "I don't think it's a good idea for you to go alone. You don't always keep your cool around Bruce."

He was right about that, but... "Everything in me says I need to make sure you stay away from him."

Scott said nothing. He folded and unfolded the tip of his right sock that hung off the ends of his toes.

Mark leaned back against the headboard and stared at the ceiling, drumming his fingers on his bent knees. "Don't ask me to do this."

"I don't think threatening him is the way to go. I think maybe he'll listen to me. More than he will you, anyway. I think…" Scott slid off the bed and went for his bag by the closet across the room. He crouched and searched inside, shoving aside item after item until he tugged out a pair of jeans. "I think after I sort of stood up to him in the alley, Bruce might actually like me. Or at least respect me in his own twisted way."

Mark could see that. Anyone who bothered to talk to Scott would have no choice but to like him.

Scott pulled off the pajama pants and slid on his jeans, looking so determined and serious.

Mark sighed. "Well, we're not going now."

"Huh?"

He pointed at the jeans. "It's the middle of the night. Why are you getting dressed?"

"Oh." Scott glanced down. "I don't know." He laughed and went to unbutton his jeans, then froze. "Wait. We? You're okay with us both going?"

"Okay with it?" Mark snorted out a laugh. "Hardly." He folded his arms over his chest and stretched his legs out in front of him. "There's nothing about you being close to Kreger that I'm okay with. But I think you're probably right about me losing my cool and him listening better to you." He paused, wanting to get his next words right. "I know I said this before, but I'm really not into telling you what to do. I just… I don't want you to get hurt. I don't like how I've reacted to this whole Bruce thing. You promised me you'd stay away from him, and I'm mad at myself for getting so pissed when you didn't keep that promise."

"I should've talked to you about my idea to follow him."

"Me too. I'm used to doing things on my own, in my own way."

Scott approached the end of the bed. "That's because you didn't have anyone to count on." He crawled onto the mattress and up Mark's body on all fours. "You may have slept with more guys than me. You may have even been serious with a few of them." He settled his ass on Mark's thighs. "But you've always been alone."

Mark sucked in a quick breath. Now that he knew what it was like to get serious with someone, he couldn't deny he'd never come close with anyone before Scott. He'd cared about Dale, but what he was feeling for Scott went beyond that.

Scott unfolded Mark's arms from across his chest. "You once told me I'd been waiting a long time to get what I needed. You were waiting too." He leaned in and kissed the side of Mark's neck, a soft brush of lips that brought out a shudder. "You were waiting for me." Another kiss.

This was a side of Scott he hadn't seen before. Bold. Confident. At least when it came to the two of them being together.

Mark laid his hands on Scott's lower back and tugged him closer. "You should be a psych major." He'd probably already read more books on the subject than every psychology undergrad did during their entire time in the school's program.

Scott shook his head and nuzzled Mark's neck. "I don't always understand people. How they act, why they want what they want, how they treat other people."

"Me either."

How anyone could joke about hurting Scott like Bruce had done with his friends before the fight in the alley was beyond comprehension.

Scott sat back. He held Mark's face and kissed him. So sensual. The way he always touched Mark, but now Scott lacked the nervousness he'd had in every move he'd made when they'd first met. Mark could get used to this.

Another kiss, and Scott pulled back. "So we'll go see Bruce together?"

"Yeah." At this point, refusing him anything wasn't much of a possibility. "Here." Mark shifted, signaling for him to get up. He gripped the front of Scott's jeans. "Take these off." He crossed the room and went to the dresser. He emptied two drawers, dumping his clothes into a laundry basket on the floor. He picked up Scott's duffel bag, handed it to him, and pointed to the drawers. "Put your clothes in there."

Scott stared at the open, now empty drawers, clutching his bag to his chest, his eyes wide, his mouth hanging open. That nervous innocence was back.

Mark laughed. "Don't freak on me. It's not an engagement ring." He leaned in and held Scott's chin in one hand. "It doesn't have to mean anything. Okay? Just that I want you to stay. Bruce or no Bruce."

But that did mean something, didn't it? He took a chance and headed back to the bed, leaving Scott alone at the dresser. Sometimes Scott needed to think things through, and Mark didn't want it to seem like he was pressuring him.

A few minutes later, he heard the drawers shut; then Scott slid into the bed alongside him. He wore the flannel pajama pants again. "Thank you."

Mark turned so they were face-to-face. "You're welcome."

"Not just for the drawers." Scott bit his lower lip and kept his gaze locked on Mark's chest.

"Hey." Mark leaned in and took Scott's lip between his teeth. He lightly tugged until Scott released it. He kissed him, dragging his tongue over that lower lip. "Tell me."

"Thank you for respecting what I think about how to handle Bruce."

Mark gave a nod. He slid over onto him until Scott's body was flat against the mattress, his legs spread wide, making room for Mark.

"Thank *you* for everything." Mark swallowed down the emotion welling in his throat. Hadn't they done enough talking already tonight? There were other ways to show Scott he appreciated him. He slid a hand under the bottom of Scott's shirt, over his stomach, raising the shirt as he made his way up. When he reached a nipple and teased it with the edge of his thumb, Scott gasped.

Mark took Scott's wrists in both hands and forced his arms over his head. He pressed the backs of his hands to the mattress. That was when he saw them.

What the hell?

He bolted upright, lifting Scott's arms as he went, examining each wrist. "Are these from the cuffs?"

"Yeah." Scott smiled.

A fucking smile? This wasn't anything smile-worthy.

"Guess I was moving around too much."

Mark's stomach rolled. How had he missed that? How had he not known?

The smile faded from Scott's face. "Mark, it's okay."

Okay? He couldn't stop staring at Scott's arms. And the bruises on each. Fucking *bruises*.

"It's not a big deal," Scott added.

"You should've told me."

"They don't hurt." He wrapped a hand around one wrist and squeezed. "See. My skin's just always been sensitive, and I was tugging on them pretty hard."

Mark examined each arm more closely. "You sure they don't hurt?"

"Positive. And..."

"What?"

"It was kinda cool seeing them the next day, remembering how intense the weekend was." He ran a palm over Mark's cheek. "Please don't be upset. It's nothing like Dale. I loved every moment of it. Okay?"

Mark saw the genuine concern and honesty in his eyes. "Okay."

He'd never been into inflicting serious pain on anyone, and after that night with Dale, he had thought seeing something like this on Scott would just about kill him. But knowing Scott didn't mind had Mark seriously conflicted. Now that the panic had passed, he couldn't deny that the reminder of what they'd done was turning him on. Which probably shouldn't have surprised him. He'd always loved seeing a guy's red ass after being thoroughly spanked and fucked.

Not that too many guys had been into the spanking thing before Scott. Not the way Scott had.

Which had a delicious thought running through his head. Could he get Scott to come simply by spanking that gorgeous ass?

Scott stretched and yawned.

Mark filed the idea away for later. He lay down and pulled a sleepy Scott close. Maybe if the talk with Bruce went well, that was how they could celebrate.

That was if he didn't blow it by freaking when it came time to tie Scott up again. He closed his eyes and tried to convince himself he wouldn't. He had to trust what Scott said. He didn't want to ruin the amazing thing they had going when it came to the sex. He wouldn't do that to Scott.

Scott settled in again with his head on Mark's chest.

Mark ran a hand down his back. "Are you sure…"

"Absolutely."

Okay. He could do this. He could trust Scott.

* * *

Mark summoned what little patience he had left and leaned against the hall wall beside Scott. They were on the first floor of the Sampson Science Building, and the class inside the Geology room was running long.

It had taken all day to find a time when they could get Bruce alone. He and his football teammates had spent the afternoon at a special weight lifting session, so Mark had settled on catching Bruce after his night class. His roommates had mentioned it was one of the rare classes Bruce never missed and that he'd be there until nine p.m.

It was five after.

A minute later, the door finally opened. The first student out was Bruce. He stopped in the doorway when he spotted them. "What the fuck do you want?"

Mark held back the reaction to lay into the asshole, and instead waited for Scott to give it a go like he'd promised.

"We just want to talk," Scott said.

Students exited the classroom, squeezing past Bruce on their way out. He didn't make a move to give any of them more room to get by. The last one to leave was the professor, who wasn't about to do the squeeze-by routine. He cleared his throat, and Bruce stepped aside an inch, maybe two. The professor gave in and left, giving a nod to Mark and Scott as he walked by.

Mark gestured with a tilt of his head to the empty classroom. "Let's take this inside."

Scott nodded but didn't go in, most likely holding back until Bruce went inside first. Smart move. Bruce was probably just waiting for either of them to get in his face.

"Just to talk," Scott reassured Bruce. "It won't take long."

"Fine." He stalked back into the classroom.

The room was designed for student labs and was smaller than the ones that held hundreds of students for lectures taught by the same tired tenured professors year after year. The walls were lined with shelves behind glass doors, each shelf showcasing samples of rocks and crystals. Mark leaned against the edge of one of the counter-height black tables, keeping his feet firmly planted on the ground as he waited.

Bruce stood with his back to the wall at the front of the class, not far from the door. "I don't have time for your shit. Why don't you go have a chat with the cops? I'm sure they got more questions for you."

Mark took a steadying breath. "I'm pretty sure you don't want me to do that."

Scott threw Mark a pointed look from where he stood at the far end of the desk, and Mark got that he should stop talking now.

Scott refocused on Bruce. "We just wanted to see if we could work something out so no one gets into any more trouble."

"Trouble?" Bruce scoffed, then spoke to Mark again. "Your ass is so gettin' kicked out of this school. You shouldn't have messed with me."

"Seriously? Are you that stupid?" Mark shoved away from the desk and tugged out his phone. He held it up in front of Bruce's face so he could see the last picture he'd taken: Bruce on his knees giving a big, bald, tattooed guy head. "When everyone finds out how you've lied, you're the one who's going to be sorry."

Bruce stared at the phone. His jaw clenched; his nostrils flared.

"Why, you asshole." He didn't make a move, though. He kept his gaze locked on the phone's screen.

"Mark." Scott tugged on his arm and gave him a pleading look. After Mark took a step back and put his phone away, Scott directed his attention at Bruce again. "We're not going to tell anyone you're gay."

"I'm not a fag!" Bruce clamped his mouth shut, but there was something new in his expression. He made eye contact with Scott, and for the first time, Bruce seemed to have a certain degree of vulnerability to him. No matter how or when it happened, accepting that people were going to know you were gay, that you loved cock, could be a very difficult thing for any guy. Mark would've felt bad for him if he'd been anyone else.

Then the expression returned to the anger Bruce usually sported, and he stormed past Scott to the far side of the classroom. He stared into one of the glass cabinets at the rocks and crystals in various shapes and colors that lined the shelves. Grays and pinks and greens. Some sparkling and others almost glowing. Who knew rocks could be so damn pretty? Bruce was most likely not seeing the beauty before him, or in his own situation. Too bad. For many guys coming out was the most freeing experience of their lives.

Bruce just stood there, his entire body shifting with each breath. There was no way he was going to admit he was gay, let alone admit to all that he'd done to Mark.

Scott stepped toward him, going slowly, inch by inch, like Bruce was a wild horse he'd spook if he made any sudden movements.

"Scott," Mark warned. He wanted him to stop, wanted him to do his talking from as far away from Bruce as he could manage. That was why he'd suggested the more open classroom instead of having this talk in the narrow hallway.

"It's okay," Scott said, his attention still glued on Bruce's back. "It's okay to be gay. It doesn't make you less of a man."

"Shut the fuck up. I'm not—" He didn't finish that time.

"It's okay." Scott was getting too close. "It's going to be okay."

Mark started to move so he could get in between them. Scott put a hand up, silently asking him to stop.

Reluctantly Mark nodded.

Scott started inching forward once more. "You had to know everyone would find out you lied about Mark. What were you thinking would happen?"

Bruce said nothing.

"Do you want them to kick you out of school? Do you want to get thrown off the football team? Get arrested for messing with the cops? Do you want everyone to know you're gay?"

Again, nothing. Which said a lot.

Mark hadn't even considered that. But it made sense. Bruce couldn't have thought he'd get away with such a ridiculous lie, which meant, even if it had been subconscious, he was hoping people would find out.

"Shut up." Those two words lacked the punch Bruce had said them with earlier. He smacked his palms against the glass doors before him. The doors rattled but didn't break. "I don't wanna get thrown off the team. I got a whole fuckin' year left."

"Maybe," Scott said, "you won't get kicked off. If you come clean about everything."

"No. I'll be in a shit-load of trouble. And I can't…I can't say why."

Now they were getting somewhere. Mark wanted to know what the hell was driving Bruce, why he'd really lied to the cops.

Maybe Scott already knew. He took another step. "It's okay. If you accept yourself, accept who you are, you could have healthier relationships."

Mark couldn't resist. "You know, one where the guy uses lube and doesn't just think about his own dick plowing into your ass."

Scott threw Mark another look that said he wasn't helping.

Mark shrugged and gestured for Scott to continue.

"You don't have to be with guys who treat you like shit. You don't have to hide what you want. If you like it rough, I mean, if you're into the rough thing in bed, there are guys who'll go there with you who aren't assholes about your safety." Scott gave Mark a smile. Mark couldn't help but return it.

Bruce had turned his head and was watching their exchange over his shoulder. He removed his hands from the doors and whispered his next words. "I was…"

When he didn't say more, Scott asked, "You were what?"

"I don't know. You two made me…mad. When I saw you together I was…"

"Jealous?"

He kept his back to them in silence for what felt like an eternity, then finally said, "I guess."

"What?" Mark wasn't sure he wanted to take this conversation any further.

Bruce faced them and flung an arm through the air, wildly

gesturing at them. "I watched you two doin' all kinds of weird, kinky shit."

"And you liked what we were doing?" Scott asked.

Bruce nodded. "The more shit I saw you guys doin', the more I added to what I'd told the cops." He clenched his mouth shut again.

Mark moved in. "You're an asshole. You're jealous of what he and I have together, so you try to destroy me, destroy my future? How juvenile could you be?"

Scott put a hand on his arm. "Mark, don't."

Mark breathed deep and stepped back.

Bruce glanced from one to the other. "Who the hell's in charge in your…" He gestured between them again. "In your thing?"

Scott's brow furrowed as he looked to Mark, then back to Bruce. "It's a relationship, and neither of us is in charge."

Bruce snorted out a laugh. "He sure orders your ass around a lot for not bein' the boss of you."

That made it official. This guy was an idiot. Hadn't he been paying attention? If anyone was leading this moment, it was Scott.

"That's the thing," Scott said. "You don't have to be ashamed of the kind of kink you like with your sex. It doesn't mean you're not in charge of your own life. So you want some big, tough guy to get rough with you? For him to shove you face-first over the arm of your couch and take you from behind while he holds you down?"

Bruce's breathing picked up again. Not from anger this time.

Yeah, what Scott had described was definitely what he wanted.

"So what?" Scott added. "It's an incredibly hot way to get laid." He waited until Bruce met his gaze. "That doesn't mean you deserve to be disrespected by the guys who fuck you—or that you should disrespect yourself."

"That's choice comin' from you." He reached out and brushed Scott's wrist above the lingering marks poking out the cuff of his long-sleeve shirt.

That did it. Mark shoved Bruce against the glass-encased shelves. The doors rattled, and the rocks teetered inside. "Don't you ever touch him again."

For once Bruce didn't return the assault. He glanced at Scott over Mark's shoulder. "You know you can do better than this asshole, right?"

Mark shoved him again. "God, you're a fucking idiot. We came here to help you."

"Stop." Scott put a hand on Mark's shoulder and encouraged him back a few steps. He spoke to Bruce again. "What Mark and I do is private and none of your business. And it doesn't matter what you saw or if you think we've done anything wrong or weird. All that matters is that he and I are doing what makes us feel good. It's no one else's business to judge. If you like the idea of getting held down or spanked or whipped or flogged or whatever, there are places you can go to meet guys who are into that stuff."

That had Bruce's attention again. "Where?"

Scott opened his mouth to speak but said nothing. He looked Mark's way.

"I don't know. I've never been anywhere like that." Despite the surprise that he was actually about to do this, Mark had to follow Scott's lead. "I've got a friend I could ask."

Bruce stared at him, then Scott again. "Why you guys doin' this? Sayin' this shit to me?"

Finally, they were getting somewhere. Mark let a smile form. "Because you're going to tell the cops the truth."

Bruce shook his head. He took a step forward, and Mark moved in his way before Bruce could get any closer to Scott.

"Get out of my way. I'm just thinkin'." He stepped around them and wandered the perimeter of the room, browsing the shelves of rocks and crystals as if he was looking for a specific one. He stopped. "It'll be all over campus. No matter what you were thinkin' about me, I don't wanna get kicked out of school. I wanna keep playin' football. My dad played when he went here. It's a big deal to him that I'm on the team. I can't let him down."

"You think they'll kick you off the team for being gay?" Scott asked.

"No. For lyin' to the cops."

"Because you weren't sexually assaulted?"

Mark held back the smug smile that wanted out. Scott was on a roll. Getting Bruce to admit the truth here in private would go a long way to getting him to say it to anyone else.

Bruce rolled his eyes. "You already know I lied about it. After the fight in the alley with him"—he gestured to Mark but kept talking to Scott—"I was all keyed up. I went to see this guy I know. I let him…" He hesitated, then shrugged. "I let him fuck me. Afterwards he made some smart-ass remark about the bruises from the fight, said I shouldn't use my face to catch a football. That's when I figured I'd go to the cops, make it sound like the alley was more than it was."

Scott nodded. He had his gaze locked on the floor before him like he was in deep thought. Then he snapped his fingers and pointed at Bruce. "If we explain things right, it'll show how scared you were to come out. The big *football star* having to tell everyone he's gay. All that pressure had you making some bad choices."

"Fuck that. I'm not sayin' that."

"But I think it'll work. And the reaction won't be what you think it will. You're going to have so many people on this campus pulling for you—the jock who's brave enough to come out."

Mark had been "out" for years and no one had ever told him he was brave. The university would probably institute a yearly pride parade in Bruce Kreger's honor.

Mark kept his mouth shut on that note. Scott was close to getting Bruce to agree to take back all his accusations.

Bruce considered Scott for another moment. "Nah." He shook his head. "I can't do that. I'm not tellin' the cops nothin'." He made for the door.

"Wait." Mark paused a moment, trying to find a way to talk himself out of this. But it was the best option, and Scott had gotten them this far. "I'll go with you. You tell them the truth, and I'll say I don't want to file charges. You might be able to walk away from this without getting in trouble."

"Why would you do that?"

Mark met Scott's gaze. "I'm beginning to see that doing the right thing isn't always the same as doing what feels right."

Scott gave him an impressed smile.

He could get lost in that look. But he had something else to say.

He marched over to Bruce and jabbed a finger at him. "But I'm keeping those pictures in case you change your mind. And let me tell you. It's one thing to admit you're gay. It's a whole other to see the evidence of how much you love sucking cock plastered all over Facebook. I'll do what I can to help keep you out of trouble, but you are to stay away from me and Scott. That's the deal. Take it or leave it."

Bruce paced the room again, back to nonchalantly browsing the rocks and crystals like Mark's entire future wasn't in the balance. He finally stopped. "Deal." Despite that one word, he seemed more pissed off than when they'd entered the room.

"Okay. Meet me outside the police station tomorrow at ten."

Bruce left the classroom without another word.

Mark stared at the door as it closed behind Bruce. "You handled that well."

"Thanks." Scott came to stand at his side. "I was nervous."

"It didn't show."

Scott laughed at that. "Maybe I should apply for a job getting criminals to confess." The way he'd said the words, he'd obviously meant it as a joke.

Mark pictured him as a masked, cape-wearing crime-fighter in one of those comics he loved to read. The image fit.

It wasn't the lawyers or the cops or the university conduct board who were going to save Mark.

It was Scott.

He reached sideways and took Scott's hand in his. "Thanks for doing this."

"You're welcome."

"Do you think he'll tell the truth?"

"I don't know," Scott said. "Maybe you should have your lawyer there tomorrow, just in case."

"Yeah. Good idea."

They were quiet for a long moment.

"I want to believe him," Scott whispered.

"Me too. Guess we'll know for sure tomorrow."

* * *

Scott sprinted up the staircase of Mark's apartment building, taking the steps two at a time. He couldn't wait to hear what had happened at the police station. Mark hadn't so much as sent a text to let him know if Bruce had shown up or not.

Scott had originally planned to go with them, but Mark hadn't wanted him to miss any of his classes. Reluctantly Scott had agreed, and he'd headed to his ten o'clock class at the same time as Mark had gone to the police station. Since then, Scott hadn't heard a word.

He hurried up the last flight of stairs. The overhead lights were off, and in the darkness his wet sneakers slipped on a step. He almost toppled over onto his ass. He caught himself on the railing just in time. His clothes and hair were also drenched from the rain, even with the umbrella he'd borrowed from Mark. It had been raining for days, and there seemed to be no end in sight.

At Mark's floor, he took off down the hall for the apartment door but found it locked.

Not a good sign. Mark should've been home long before him. Scott's last class had run late, and he'd had to walk all the way across campus since the university shuttle had been full of students.

He slid his backpack off. He'd just get out one of his books, have a seat, and wait. And of course try not to worry.

A charge of lightning lit up the sky outside the window at the end of the hallway past Mark's apartment. A man stood before the window.

What little light there was coming from behind him kept his face veiled in shadows. Another flash of lightning brightened the hallway for a split second. The quick view of Bruce's face showed he was clearly upset. He wore a university sweatshirt with the school's angry, snarling bulldog mascot on the front. He had the hood pulled up over his head, casting his face in even more shadows.

"Bruce? Is everything okay?"

He crept forward. "Your roommates said you were stayin' with some guy. I figured it was Mark."

Scott wasn't sure he'd ever heard Bruce call Mark by his name before. Usually he just called him asshole.

"How'd it go today?"

Bruce shrugged. "What does it matter?"

"It matters to you. To me too."

Bruce paused for a second, then took another step. "Thanks."

"What are you doing here?" Mark's voice filled the hall. He was headed toward them, just as drenched as Scott. Surprisingly he didn't make a move toward Bruce. He stopped behind Scott. "I told you after today you were to stay away from us."

"Just wanted to talk to him before I took off. Didn't want him thinkin' I blamed him."

"Blamed me for what?" Scott asked. This wasn't sounding good.

Bruce shook his head. "It's nothin'. Just wanted to say thanks for gettin' me to see this had to end."

Scott gave a nod. "You're leaving?"

"Yeah."

Now that Bruce was closer, the defeated expression was obvious. He looked so different from the guy who had first kicked Scott out of his chair at the library.

"Why are you leaving? What happened?"

"I'll let your"—Bruce tilted his head toward Mark—"whatever he is to you fill you in." He shoved his hands in the pockets of his sweatshirt and strode past them.

When he was gone down the stairs, Scott asked, "What happened?"

"A lot." Mark unlocked the door and went to turn on the light, but the apartment remained in the dark. "Power must be out." He stepped inside. "I think I've got candles somewhere in my bedroom closet."

Scott followed him in. Lightning flashed again outside, momentarily lighting up the room and Mark's back as he walked away. Scott set the umbrella by the door with his backpack. "Mark, what happened?"

Mark stopped before he made it across the room to the hallway. "He recanted just like he said he would. Said he'd lied about everything."

"What did the police do?"

"Hang on." Mark left the room. He returned with a stash of candles and a towel for each of them. He lit the candles. They stripped off their soaking wet clothes until they stood naked in the dancing flickers of light.

"Come here." Mark held open a towel. Scott stepped forward, and Mark wrapped him in the terrycloth, drying him off at the same time as holding him. When Scott was nearly dry, Mark rubbed the towel over Scott's hair.

He laughed at that. "I'm dry enough." He reached for the other towel and did the same for Mark, but Mark was still shivering. Scott took him by the hand and led him to the couch. He retrieved the balled up blanket from the far end, and they got under it together.

"Okay," Scott said. "What happened?"

"He told them I didn't hurt him, that we didn't even have sex."

"They believed him?"

"Yeah. Without a lot of trouble too, so I'm guessing they were doubting his story to begin with."

"So you're in the clear?"

"Yeah."

Scott lunged forward and hugged Mark. "I knew it was all going to work out okay."

"For the most part."

Scott pulled back, afraid to ask for details but needing to know. "What's going to happen to Bruce?"

Mark didn't respond. His face was masked by the darkness the low light of the candles couldn't completely diminish. There was something he didn't want to admit.

"He's…" Mark sucked in a deep breath and spoke again in a rush of words. "He's kicked out of school. The conduct board wasn't too thrilled with his blatant lies about something so serious."

"Shit."

"Yeah. No more college. No more football. It'll be all over campus, online. I have a feeling a lot of students will rally around him for coming out, like you said, but it'll probably be too late to change the decision."

"So that's what he meant about not blaming me? But I talked him into it."

"Hey. Don't go there. This was all his doing. He chose to concoct this ridiculous lie."

"I guess. But you're all cleared of everything?"

"Yeah. The conduct board said they'd let the fight go since there were extenuating circumstances."

"I guess you were right about talking to him. I'm not sure how else we would've gotten the cops to believe us."

"*Threatening* him was my idea. *Talking to him* was yours. You were very convincing."

"I just wish it was over for everybody."

"Don't worry too much about him. He's still an asshole, and his dad brought in a high-priced attorney who's claiming Bruce was under so much stress that he snapped. They're trying to get the police not to bring any charges against him. But in any case, he's done at this school." Mark let out a long sigh and leaned back, his head resting on the couch behind him. "I'm just relieved this is all over." He reached out and settled a hand at the back of Scott's neck. "Come here."

"But…"

"What?"

"I feel like we should do something to help him."

"I'm not sure there's anything we can do. With all the national attention the school's gotten in the past, it's likely they're just going to let him go home with his dad, anything to quietly end this."

"Do you think he'll end up blaming us at some point?"

"Not you. Me? Definitely. But in the long run, I think he'll see he could've gotten in a lot more trouble if he'd taken this any further. Honestly, he looked relieved. We gave him the push to do what he'd been wanting to do—to come out—and I think he's going to have a lot to deal with on his own. His dad was seriously pissed."

"What a way to come out to your dad."

"Yeah." Mark slid closer to bury his face in Scott's neck. "Do you have a lot of homework tonight?"

"Uh-uh."

"Good. I know just how I want to celebrate."

He kissed Scott. A long, deep kiss that Scott felt all the way through him. Mark's skin smelled of the rain, but the cold was long gone. The warmth of him enveloped Scott, and his own skin tingled everywhere in response. Mark worked a hand under the blanket, ran it down Scott's stomach. He gripped his cock, stroking and teasing and kissing him until he had Scott hard and shifting his hips with each slide of Mark's fist along his shaft.

Then Mark pulled back. Before Scott could catch his breath after that searing kiss, Mark threw off the blanket and tugged him off the couch. He grabbed him by the hips and spun him around. Mark pressed against his back and walked them as one to the far end of the couch. He whispered in Scott's ear. "Bend over." He didn't wait for him to comply. He shoved him forward over the arm of the couch and forced Scott's legs apart. "Hands on the couch over your head."

Scott did as he was told, desire blazing through him at the commanding voice behind him.

Mark reached between his legs and cupped Scott's balls in one hand. "Don't move." He smacked Scott's ass with his free hand. Massaging his balls, he slapped his ass again. "Tell me how this makes you feel."

"I…I don't know."

"Yes, you do." He smacked again, heating up Scott's other ass cheek. "Use your words. You're a writer."

"I feel… I don't know… I feel alive. Special."

He let go of Scott's balls and leaned over his back, pressing his half-hard cock between Scott's ass cheeks. "Because you're mine."

The whispered words thrilled Scott as much as the touches.

"I'm going to fuck you right here over the couch. Just like I know you want."

"Please."

"But not right now." Mark straightened. "Not this time."

"Please."

Another smack to his ass. "No."

Smack.

"This time I want something else. I'm going to keep this up until you're ready to pop."

Another smack.

"You will tell me when you're close, and you will not come until my lips are wrapped around your dick. Got it?"

Scott whimpered. He was almost there already.

Smack.

His ass had to be beet red. What would it feel like to have Mark's hands clenching his hot ass while he blew him? He whimpered again. "Please."

Smack.

"Got it? Not a drop of cum until you're in my mouth."

"Yes, yes. I promise. Please."

Smack.

A knock sounded on the door.

Mark stopped.

Whoever was at the door knocked again.

He groaned and leaned over Scott's back. His hot, heavy breaths hit the back of Scott's neck. "It's probably my neighbor."

Another knock.

"She keeps getting my mail delivered to her place. I saw her downstairs earlier, so she knows I'm home." He stood. "I'll get rid of her." He shifted Scott around to the front of the couch. "Sit. Carefully. Keep that ass warm for me."

Scott nodded and sat, his skin hot against the plush cushion.

Mark wrapped the blanket around his own waist and went to the door. Keeping his body positioned behind the door, he opened it a crack.

"I'm looking for my son, Scott Murphy."

"Dad?" Scott jumped off the couch and lunged for his soaked jeans. He hurried to jerk them on, taking care as the wet fabric slid over his heated ass and his flagging erection. He scrambled for the door when Mark opened it the rest of the way.

His dad entered, looking none too happy.

"Dad, how did you—"

"Your roommates said you'd moved out. Owen at the coffee shop told me where to find this place." He threw a heated look Mark's way. "I'm guessing it was your idea that my son lie to me?"

"No," Scott said. "Dad, I—"

"Not telling me you're living with someone is lying. The kind of man who encourages you to lie to me is not good enough for you."

It wasn't hard to miss the clench of Mark's jaw. He didn't react, though. His voice was neutral when he said, "I should go put on some clothes."

"Yeah, you do that." Scott's dad turned his back on Mark.

Mark gave Scott a look, part apology, part worry, part support, then headed for his bedroom.

After the bedroom door shut, his dad opened his mouth as if to say something else but gasped instead. He gripped Scott by the elbows and held his arms up, examining one wrist, then the other. The slight bruising was almost gone, but it was still obvious enough, even in the low light of the candles. And with the way the marks had faded, they looked like fingerprints wrapped around Scott's arms.

"Did he do this to you?"

"It's not—"

"Go get your things, Scott. You're not staying here."

Chapter Eight

A flash of lightning lit up the room, immediately followed by a crack of thunder that tore through the small apartment.

Scott stood frozen in place. He'd never heard his dad sound so pissed off.

"Dad, it's nothing."

"Nothing?" He reached for Scott's arm again. "He's hurting you."

"No!" Scott kept his gaze locked on the floor. He so didn't want to explain this. "Please don't ask." That was when the lights decided to turn back on. Perfect timing. Out of the corner of his eye, Scott could see his dad intensely watching him.

"Is he hurting you?"

Scott shook his head.

"Is someone else?"

"No." He crossed the room and dropped onto the couch. His still-heated ass stung with the action. He held back the wince.

His dad came to sit next to him. "What happened?" He examined Scott's wrists again, more closely this time. "This is from being tied up."

"Please. Can we just drop it? You're my *dad*."

"That's why I have to know."

"But it's embarrassing talking about this with you."

"I'm sorry about that, but we are not going to drop it. Mark did this to you?"

Oh God. What was he supposed to say?

"He ties you up?"

Scott nodded.

His dad didn't say anything more right away. Hopefully he'd decided to let the completely embarrassing conversation go.

Or not.

More softly he asked, "It's something you want him to do?"

Yet again, Scott couldn't find the words.

"I have to know, Scott. Is this from him doing something you wanted?"

"Yes."

"It's something you enjoy?"

There was no getting out of admitting the truth. He swallowed, then spoke again in a rush. "Yes."

"Does he hit you?"

He could still feel the warm sting of Mark's hand on him. He searched for the right words. "He doesn't hurt me." He dropped his head and buried his face in his hands. His next words were muffled. "Can we not talk about this?"

There was a long pause, and then his dad said, "It's okay." He ran a comforting hand over Scott's back, then sank back farther on the couch. "In fact, your mother liked that sort of thing."

"Dad!" Scott lifted his head but still couldn't face him.

"Oh, I forgot. Parents don't have sex." He could tell his dad was smiling now. "She was a wonderful person. Having a lot in common with her is not a bad thing."

"I know." He always loved when his dad compared him to her. He wouldn't let what they were talking about change that reaction.

"I should've guessed when I saw those marks. She bruised easily like you. It's just... I worry about you."

"Mark is a really good guy. He cares about me."

"I can see that."

Scott looked at his dad for the first time since moving to the couch. He was staring off toward the end of the hallway.

Mark stood there, now fully dressed, concern evident in the confused expression on his face. "Is everything okay?"

"Yeah." Scott tried to keep his voice even, despite the awkwardness of the moment. "Everything's fine."

Mark nodded. "Okay. I'll let you two talk." He hesitated like it was taking all his effort to walk away. He gave Scott another nod and headed back down the hall for his room.

After the door closed, his dad said, "I trust you. I trust your judgment. But I need you to promise me one thing. That you'll never let him or anyone else do something you don't want. No matter what you feel for him. And if it becomes too much, if it's changing into something you don't want and you don't know how to walk away, you'll come talk to me."

"I promise. Can we not talk about this anymore?"

"All right," he said with a laugh. "Besides, I came to talk about this." He pulled out an envelope from his inside jacket pocket and handed it over. "You told me to open any mail about your schooling in case it was important. I figured this qualified." The return address indicated it was from the Creative Writing Graduate Program at NYU. "You were accepted into the Advanced Writer's Fellowship."

"What?" Scott couldn't hold back the excited tone. He slid the letter out of the envelope and read the first line congratulating him. "I got in?"

"You did."

"I got in." And not just in the Master's Program, but the fellowship that was designed for *students who showed exceptional promise.*

"Congratulations." Pride was overflowing in that one word. "I'm surprised, though. I didn't know you had applied."

"One of my professors suggested it. I didn't want to disappoint him. He's been really great to me." He kept reading over the first line of the letter.

"I thought you were pretty set on Michigan State."

"I…" He set the letter on his thigh. "I am."

His dad said nothing for a moment, studying Scott. "This program at NYU sounds wonderful. The guest author lectures alone look phenomenal. Seems like a great opportunity. Once-in-a-lifetime even."

It hurt to be reminded of what he was giving up, but he could do this for his dad. He hadn't even freaked over the bruises.

"I'm going to grad school in Michigan." He wasn't about to head off hundreds of miles away to another program, leaving his dad all alone again.

"Listen, there's something—" His dad's words came to an abrupt stop.

Mark stood at the end of the hall again. "Sorry. Didn't mean to interrupt. I thought I heard yelling."

"No," Scott said, "we're fine." Fine? He couldn't stop staring at the acceptance letter. They picked him. *Him.*

A moment later, he felt Mark's comforting touch on his chin. He ran a thumb along his jawline. "Are you okay?"

"Yeah."

Scott was caught in that look of concern on Mark's face. He wanted to tell him about being accepted to NYU. About the fellowship and how few people they accepted each year and what an honor it was to have been chosen. But he couldn't say any of that right then. If his dad heard it, he'd want him to go to New York.

His dad was watching them with an odd look. Relief, maybe. He stood and held a hand out to Mark. "Let's do this right. You must be Mark. It's nice to meet you."

"You too, sir." They shook, and Mark gestured to the door where they'd first seen each other. "That wasn't exactly how I wanted to meet you. For one, I wanted to be wearing more clothes."

"It's okay." Without letting go of Mark's hand, he added, "I don't want you to take this the wrong way, because I'm really not judging anything the two of you do together. That's your private business, but if you ever do anything to my son he doesn't want or if you ever hurt him—"

"Dad!" Scott jumped off the couch and tugged on his dad's arm until he let go of Mark. When it seemed like his dad wouldn't push the issue, Scott explained. "He saw the bruises on my wrists."

"Oh." Mark ducked his head for a moment, then stood taller, eye to eye with Scott's dad. "Mr. Murphy, you have to believe me. I would never hurt him. Not like you're implying."

They stared at each other in silence for another minute, or what felt that long to Scott.

"Okay," his dad finally offered. "My son trusts you, and I trust him." He jabbed a finger toward Mark. "Don't disappoint either of us."

Mark cracked a smile. "Deal."

"Good." His dad gestured to the couch for Scott to join him as he sat. "Now, I want to know about you two living together."

Forgetting his ass was still sensitive, Scott dropped to the cushion again. "It's not like that."

Mark had taken a seat at his desk beside the couch. He gave him a nod, and Scott continued.

"I've just been staying here instead of going back to my apartment every night. We're not *living* together." He was hoping Mark wouldn't mention why he'd come to stay, about Bruce or anything that had happened in the past few weeks. Now that it was all over with, he didn't want his dad worrying for nothing.

"You sleep here?"

Scott ran his palms over the rain-soaked jeans covering his thighs. They could stop directing every conversation back to sex anytime now. His face had to be red, probably more than his ass at that moment. "Yes, I sleep here."

"You take showers here?"

"Yeah."

"You eat here? Keep your toothbrush and your clothes here? In a closet or a drawer?"

"Yeah."

"That's living together."

Scott met Mark's gaze, unsure how Mark would define their relationship and even more unsure of how to explain it to his dad.

"Is he the reason you don't want to go to NYU?"

Mark's eyes widened. "You applied to NYU?"

"He was accepted to a prestigious writing program." To Scott his dad added, "And I want to know why you're not going."

"I just don't want to. It has nothing to do with Mark." Or did it? Michigan was closer to Seattle.

But either way, Mark would be a plane ride away.

"Mark's moving to Seattle after he graduates."

Mark leaned forward, elbows on his knees, his gaze glued to the floor before him. What was he thinking?

Scott chewed on his bottom lip and waited for someone to speak.

"I see," his dad said.

Time to change the subject. For more than one reason. Scott asked his dad, "Can you still come to the writing competition?"

"I wouldn't miss that for anything."

He sighed, finally feeling like he could breathe after everything that had happened in the past few minutes—conversations he never wanted to have, and ones he wasn't ready to have. Or was he?

"All right." His dad stood. "I'm going to get out of your hair. I just wanted you to see that letter in case you decided to change your plans for next fall." He gave Scott a pat on the shoulder, and then he and Mark shook hands again, not saying a word that time. Scott knew why. Neither felt they needed to defend themselves or their reactions.

* * *

"Your dad hates me." Mark groaned and flopped onto the couch on his back.

Scott dried the last dish and put it away in the cabinet above the microwave. After his dad had left, he'd changed into dry clothes, and then he and Mark had made something to eat, neither saying much as they ate, then washed the dishes together.

"My dad's not like that." He went to sit at the opposite end of the couch, lifting Mark's feet and setting them on his lap. It had finally stopped raining and the sun was out. The rays coming in through Mark's living room window warmed and brightened the room and gave the moment a feeling of clarity. Only Scott wasn't sure what he was supposed to be seeing. "Besides, I guess he and my mom used to…" He gestured with a hand in the air as if that would explain it.

Mark's eyebrows rose. "What?"

"You know. Do stuff like we do."

"Really?" Mark lifted up onto his elbows. "So he understood about it?"

"Yeah. Sorry he wasn't nicer to you at first."

"Don't be. He loves you and wants to keep you safe." He leaned forward. He cupped the back of Scott's neck, then ran his fingers through the hair at his nape. "I get that."

They exchanged a long look. Scott desperately wanted to ask what Mark had meant by that, but he held back.

Mark kept those amazing fingers moving through his hair, over his skin. "So, according to your dad, we're living together."

"Yeah." Scott picked at the plaid fabric on the arm of the couch, feeling completely insecure and not sure why that reaction had returned, like the first moment he'd talked to Mark.

Mark lay back on the couch, his feet over Scott's lap again. "Do you have a copy of your book with you?"

"My book?"

"Yeah. *The Hawk in the Caverns*. You said I could read it."

"Oh. Sure. I'm still not happy with the ending, though. Something isn't right about it."

Mark lifted his feet out of the way, and Scott went to retrieve his backpack.

"Maybe I can help."

"Yeah? That'd be great." He handed the pages to Mark, who immediately began reading to himself, examining each illustration in great detail.

Scott shifted on his feet. "I should just… I should go."

"Go?"

"Yeah. I'll just go to the library or something."

"No." Mark gripped him by the waist and tugged until Scott was on the couch beside him, closer this time. Mark lifted his legs to lay them over Scott's lap again. He reached for a book on his desk. "Here. Read this while you wait." It was the erotic romance he had read to Scott while he fucked him the other day.

As Mark read, Scott tried to sit still and not squirm or worry or chew his bottom lip. He tried to read but couldn't stop glancing at Mark.

Having agents and editors reading his stuff was hard enough, but he'd prepared mentally for that. He hadn't been sure how he'd feel about people he knew reading his work. Let alone Mark.

What if he hates it?

What if he thinks it's lame?

What if he doesn't say anything?

Only it didn't look like he needed to worry. Mark seemed captivated, glued to page after page.

"Oh man." Mark moved his legs off Scott and sat taller as he kept on reading.

Scott dug out some homework and tried to work on that, not accomplishing much of anything, especially the closer Mark got to the end.

"Wow." Mark set the pages on his lap. "That was..." He paused until Scott looked his way. "I figured it'd be good but...it was amazing. Better than any fiction I've read in a long time."

"Really?"

"Yeah. The drawings... And the battles with the dragons... And the ending..." He flipped through the pages again, stopping at the panels with the last battle. The largest image featured Hawk with his dragon friend Journey as they led the forces through the winding tunnels of the caves.

That was Scott's favorite part.

"You are incredibly talented."

That—and the impressed look on Mark's face—had a rush of excitement surging through Scott. "Thank you."

"There's only one thing I don't get. The part with Hawk and his lover wasn't what I expected from you."

"What do you mean?"

"His lover broke up with him before the battle. It was very dramatic, but he seemed to lose his motivation after that."

"Yeah, I didn't want him to be a dick and act like he felt nothing, but I couldn't have him be sad for too long. There was too much at stake."

"Why did you have them break up at all?"

"I don't know. I guess I was afraid it would seem too sappy if his lover stayed and they saw each other after the battle. Like cue the dramatic music and watch them hug."

"Because they'd be so relieved the other was alive?"

"Yeah."

"Love doesn't have to be sappy. You could tie it into his character arc." He huffed out a laugh. "Listen to me. Forget I said anything. This is your story." He leaned in and gave Scott a kiss on the cheek. "And it's great. It really is."

Scott was quiet for a minute, but he had to ask. "How would you tie it into his arc?"

Mark shifted to kneel on the floor before him. He laid his hands on Scott's knees. "People who have love behind them are stronger than those without it." He gripped him by the thighs and tugged him forward until Scott was straddling his lap on the floor. "They have more to fight for." He drew him even closer, and they were plastered together, Scott's legs wrapped around Mark. He slid a hand up Scott's sides, under his T-shirt. Then he removed the shirt in one fluid motion.

Scott gasped as Mark kissed his skin at the base of his neck, an openmouthed kiss that went from his neck to a nipple without stopping. He gave another long tongue-filled kiss all the way back up to Scott's ear, his warm breath drawing out goose bumps as he said, "Love makes you brave."

Oh God. Scott tilted Mark's head back and kissed him, unable to keep from showing how his words and actions affected him.

Never breaking the kiss with the movement, Mark rolled them, pinning Scott on the floor beneath him.

Scott clutched at his arms, tugging him closer, needing more of his kisses, his touches, more of Mark.

He wanted to feel every inch of Mark pressing down on him, wanted to connect with him beyond what sex or words could ever offer. Only he had no idea how to show that to him.

Mark worked Scott's pants and underwear off and threw them aside, then did the same with his own clothes. He reached into a desk drawer for lube and a condom, and when he finally pressed inside Scott, they were facing each other, Mark's hot exhales hitting the side of Scott's neck, low groans pouring out of him.

This time there was no bondage or spanking, no commands or pleas, yet it was even more intense than any other moment they'd spent together.

Mark moved inside him in a slow rhythm that had Scott's need building in an entirely new way. Just as he was about to start begging for more, Mark buried his cock all the way inside, then stilled. He leaned down like he was going to kiss him but stopped with their lips almost touching.

Scott clutched at the backs of Mark's thighs, the muscles under his palms taut with unleashed power, Mark's chest hair teasing Scott's skin with each deep breath they took.

"I'm..." Mark searched Scott's eyes. "I'm so far beyond falling for you." He didn't wait for Scott to say anything. He brought their mouths together. A long, deep kiss Scott could feel everywhere. Then another. He kissed nearly every inch of Scott's jawline and neck, exploring his body as far as he could reach with hands and lips while still staying deep inside him.

Then Mark started moving his hips again, making love to Scott this time. There was no doubt about how to describe it. The moment—and Mark's movements—increased, building and building, becoming more...

Meaningful. That was the only word that fit.

A few more deep thrusts, and Mark was capturing Scott's breath with every drive of their bodies coming together.

Scott had never been taken with such intensity, had never felt such blinding need overtake him. He'd never wanted the release so badly, but he also wanted to keep Mark buried inside him for much, much longer. Maybe until graduation day. That sounded good.

Mark kissed him again, still plunging into him with a fast jerk of his hips. "God. Scott." He thrust one last time and groaned as he came. And came.

He was still for a moment, his body draped over Scott's, and then he was shaking in Scott's arms.

Scott held him, forcing himself not to ask if the reaction was from the orgasm or something more.

Then Mark pulled back, lowering Scott's legs to the floor. He ditched the condom and crouched over him, taking the full length of his dick into his mouth with one movement, his lips caressing Scott's length with tight suction that he repeated again and again.

Scott's body stiffened, pleasure coursing through him as he climaxed, his gaze locked on where Mark's moist lips were connected to him in such an intimate way. Mark didn't let up until Scott was growing soft in his mouth.

When he finally let go, he lay there, his head on Scott's stomach, his fingers caressing the dragon tattoo.

Scott ran a hand over the back of Mark's head. He was afraid to speak, afraid he'd say too much, or not enough. He didn't want to lose this moment, lose the way he felt. And he didn't want to make a fool of himself. Not now. He ran his fingers through Mark's dark hair.

Mark dropped a kiss on his stomach. "I don't want to walk away from this." He paused. Another kiss to Scott's abs. Another. "I'm rethinking Seattle."

Scott stilled his hand. "What?"

"I can teach anywhere. I could teach in New York."

He didn't say anything, couldn't.

"I just wanted to start over somewhere, get away from my family." Another kiss. "I could do that with you. You could take that fellowship, and I could teach at a smaller college in the city." Another kiss beside Scott's navel, and he lifted up over him. "I think you're the one for me."

Scott searched his eyes, finding more conveyed there than the words Mark had just said. "How do you know for sure?"

A grin hit Mark's lips. "I know. Besides, sometimes you have to take a leap of faith even when you don't know how things will work out."

Yeah, it was like that in his book. Hawk had to trust in his own strength and take on the mountain dwellers because not trying would've been the biggest regret of his life.

Scott didn't want to regret his own choices.

Love makes you brave.

* * *

Mark sat on the floor of the popular culture library's large display area and opened the last box. He upended it and a slew of metal parts joined the others on the floor before him. So many tiny pieces—clips and brackets and screws. It was hard to imagine that after a few turns of the screwdriver, all the parts before him would create much of anything. Sometimes the bigger picture was impossible to grasp when you looked too hard at the details.

He pulled out the instructions and started reviewing the diagram. He had until the next morning to get the shelving display unit installed and stocked before the alumni tour at 8 a.m. He'd told his boss it would only take an hour or two and had agreed to work on it after his regular shift covering the information desk. Although at the rate he was working, an hour or two wouldn't cut it. He just had too many thoughts rolling through his mind.

He tossed the instructions aside and began organizing pieces. As he worked, he once again thought back to the night he and Scott last had sex on his living room floor. He had no idea where those words he'd said to Scott about love and bravery had come from, but he'd meant every single word. No moment had ever left him feeling more alive, but also vulnerable and unsure. Despite that, he didn't regret what he'd said. Not even with the way Scott had reacted to it.

After his confession about rethinking his move to Seattle, Scott had been quiet. He looked nervous and scared lying naked on the floor. So Mark hadn't pushed the topic, and they hadn't talked about it again since.

After that night Scott had buried his head in the revisions for his book, drawing and redrawing the illustrations. Every moment he wasn't studying, he was busy on the novel, working on Mark's couch, at the library, and at Owen's coffee shop. The deadline was the end of the day Friday. Scott had two days left, and it was clear by the growing pile of discarded, crumpled drawings beside the couch that he was struggling.

Mark had really done a number on him. First he'd messed with his head about his story and had shaken Scott's confidence. He shouldn't have said anything about the ending.

And he should've waited to mention not moving to Seattle. His timing really sucked.

So he'd done his best to help Scott by ordering takeout and keeping out of the way so he could work, no matter how much he longed to tie Scott to his bed and make him talk about what he wanted.

Talking about it would have to wait.

Mark forced himself to focus on the pile of bookshelf parts before him. His phone chimed with a new text message.

From Scott. Are you finished with work yet?

He texted back. No. Have to set up a display for tomorrow.

Ok. Never mind.

What's wrong? What do you need?

Nothing. Just wanted to see you.

Where are you?

Library. 1st floor.

Come upstairs to pop culture.

Library's closing.

It's ok. Come on up. Meet you at the elevator.

Five minutes later the doors opened, and Scott exited the same elevator where they had their first kiss.

That had Mark smiling like a dork. After that kiss, he'd known that one day with Scott was never going to be enough. Now he knew one semester wouldn't either.

Scott stepped up to him, looking flushed and nervous. "Hey."

"Hey." Mark leaned in and whispered, "Did riding in that elevator get you thinking about that afternoon we spent here?"

Scott nodded.

"Did just thinking about it get you hard?"

He laughed and smacked him on the arm. "No." He looked away. "Maybe. A little bit."

Mark stepped closer, dropping his voice lower. "Me too." He pressed a kiss to Scott's lips, wanting more but guessing Scott needed something else right then. "Come on." He led him inside the main room. "How are the book revisions going?"

"It's done."

He stopped. "Yeah?"

"I wanted to thank you for helping with it."

"I didn't do anything, but you're welcome."

"You were right about the ending. They shouldn't have broken up."

Mark searched his face, wondering if Scott was talking about more than his book. "I'd love to read the changes, but I'll wait until it wins the award."

Scott gave a shrug like he didn't care what happened. *Right.* "I'm trying not to get my hopes up. I took a look at the other finalists. One of the graphic novels was done by a team of two guys, Albon and Wallace. They have some self-published titles. They're really good. They've been trying to get their work picked up by a publisher for years now."

"Don't worry about it. Win or lose this one competition, you created an excellent book. You should be proud of that. You're going to find your success."

"Thanks." Scott moved to stand before a display of vintage Star Trek trading cards, most depicting the Enterprise in battles with other ships. He opened his mouth like he was going to say something, then stopped. He started again with an ease that indicated he wasn't talking about what he'd been about to say. "I'm just glad the winners don't have to give a speech."

Mark moved in behind him. "You'd do great if you had to." He rubbed his shoulders. "You want to hang here while I finish putting this display unit together?" Which would give Scott time to work up the courage to talk about what was really on his mind.

"Sure. I could help."

"Nah. It's pretty easy. Why don't you look around? I didn't get a chance to show you much last time we were here."

Scott nodded. He wandered, not really stopping to look at much. He was distracted. He definitely wanted—needed—to talk about something.

Mark put together the ends of the unit, then added a shelf, waiting.

Scott had stopped at a bookcase full of pulp magazines. He didn't say anything for a minute, just stared at the shelf of science fiction titles with their giant octopus-like aliens and terrified men and women screaming on the covers. Without turning around he said, "Mark."

"Yeah." He secured a bracket, waited again.

"I talked to Bruce."

"When?"

"Last night after you fell asleep. He called me. Wanted to apologize for everything." He moved again, then came to an abrupt stop by the catalog station. He ran a hand along the computer's keyboard like it was the most interesting thing in the room.

"What aren't you telling me?"

"I don't... I just... I can't stop thinking about something."

"What's that?"

"What you said the other night about New York. I don't want to go to school there."

Mark went to stand in front of him. "I didn't believe it when you told your dad that, and I'm not really buying it now. You want to go."

Scott traversed the room again, alternating between chewing on the side of a thumbnail and running a hand through his blond hair. "I don't think this is going to work."

"What?"

"Us. When I finish grad school, I'm moving back home to Elmore."

"I know."

"I don't want to live anywhere else." He was shaking.

"Hey." Mark went to him again.

Scott put up a hand and took a step back before Mark could get within touching distance. "Don't." He shook his head. "I was thinking. Maybe you could get your friend Gage to show you that place where guys go who are into the kinds of stuff we've been doing. You could meet someone there." He wouldn't look at him.

What the hell? "You think that's all you are to me? Someone who happens to like what I want to give? Where have you been? Were you there with me the other day on my goddamn living room floor?" He couldn't hold back on the frustration thundering through him.

"It was..."

"What?"

"It was sex."

"It was a hell of a lot more than that. At least to me."

"To me too," Scott whispered.

"Then what are you doing?"

He didn't answer that.

"Is this because your dad saw the bruises? Because he showed up when I was spanking your ass?" Mark sounded like a dick. He knew it, but he couldn't seem to keep the emotion from his voice.

Scott shook his head again. "He said he understood."

"But do you? All that stuff you said to Bruce. Do you believe it? Are you okay with what we've done together? Or are you ashamed?"

"This isn't about that."

"No?"

"No. It took me forever to get my book done. Because all I could think about was losing you or you doing something you don't really want just so we can be together." He went back to the first display case he'd stopped at, examining the slew of Enterprises in the midst of battle. "We want different futures, and what you said the other night—" He stopped midsentence and kept scrutinizing the trading cards like he'd be quizzed on them later. Was he holding back on what he wanted to say? Or what he thought he should?

"Better to walk away now? Save yourself from the pain later? Is that it?"

"Maybe." He faced Mark again. "I don't want to be the kind of guy who sits around hoping my boyfriend will give up all his dreams to be with me."

Mark's instincts told him to drag Scott to his apartment and wrap him in the bondage tape until he promised not to leave, and that scared him. The complete lack of control and respect for Scott in that one thought unnerved him more than what had happened with Dale.

"I guess..." Scott looked toward the door. "I should go."

"Fine." Anger chipped away at the pain surging through Mark. "Get your shit out of my apartment and go." He turned his back on Scott and kicked at the half-assembled shelving unit. The end that hadn't been secured yet collapsed, and the shelf clattered to the floor.

"Mark..." Scott ran a hand down the middle of Mark's back. "I don't know..." He breathed deep and started again. "I don't know what I should do."

"Don't do this." Mark spun around as he said the words.

Scott had tears in his eyes.

Mark gripped him by the arms and pressed their foreheads together. Softer he repeated, "Don't do this." He took a chance and kissed him, caressing the sides of his face with his thumbs, pouring more than he could say with words in the press of their lips. "Don't go. We'll figure something out. Just don't go. Okay?"

Scott wrapped his arms around Mark's neck and nodded.

"I meant what I said about moving," Mark added. "Fuck Seattle. It's just a goddamn city. We can figure something out."

"Okay." Scott held on tighter, burying his face in Mark's neck. "Okay."

Mark held him in return, unsure he could let go anytime soon, and even more unsure if he'd done the right thing where Scott was concerned.

* * *

Mark keyed in the search and hit the enter button on his laptop. Ten minutes of browsing the results, and his stomach was in knots. He glanced up from his desk to the far end of the couch where Scott had been sitting hours earlier. Books and papers were still strewn all over the cushions and coffee table. Scott had been scrambling to finish the homework he'd fallen behind on while reworking his book for the competition.

Of course Mark knew it was about more than the homework. Scott had been keeping busy so he didn't have time to think about the Breakout Writer Award. The conference was underway, and later that day they'd be announcing the award winners. Scott had left a while ago to attend a workshop at the conference.

Mark refocused on his search. He'd gotten online as a distraction from his own nervousness—about the awards and his rescheduled dissertation defense, about him and Scott and their futures.

So much for a distraction. Instead of browsing Facebook, he'd gone looking for something else. Now the search results were adding to his unease.

The town of Elmore, Michigan, was home to 2,105 residents and included eight manufacturing factories, a diner, a dollar department store, and enough taverns so every citizen had a seat for happy hour.

Just like where he grew up.

And nothing like where he wanted to live.

He glanced at the books on the couch again. Could he do this for Scott? Would he end up resenting him? Or was there a chance he could be happy anywhere so long as he was with him?

A knock at the door interrupted his thoughts. He answered it and found Scott's dad standing in the hall, his face locked in a serious frown.

"You and I have to talk."

Chapter Nine

Scott's dad didn't wait for Mark to say anything. He stormed into the apartment, crossing the room in a quick series of frustrated strides. He stopped before the couch, his back straight and his body held tight.

Mark shut the door. "Mr. Murphy—"

"Let's drop the Mr. stuff. It's Craig." He faced him and in a softer tone added, "After all, you're in love with my son."

There was no way Mark could deny that. He didn't want to. "I am."

Craig nodded. "One look between the two of you and I knew. My son has always had a big heart. I knew if he met the right man..." He shook his head as if he couldn't say the rest.

"What is it you think I've done wrong?"

"It's not like that. I'm not blaming you." With a sigh he dropped onto the couch. "I'm afraid my son is making choices that aren't about what's best for him or what he wants, but are about what he thinks he should do." He gave Mark a pointed look. "Those can be very different things. He wants to attend that program at NYU."

"I know he does." Mark desperately wanted to pace the room, let out some of his frustration, but instead he went to sit beside Craig. "I tried to talk to him about it. He says he's not going."

"When I was here before, I could tell he was holding back for some reason."

"You think it's because of me?"

"I think he's waiting to see what you end up doing for sure. He tends to put his own wants and needs last."

"I told him the other night I wanted to skip Seattle, that I could go to New York with him instead."

Craig threw him a questioning stare. "What did he say?"

"He tried to break up with me."

"Oh." With that, he leaned forward, elbows on his thighs, lost in thought as he stared at the coffee table before him. Abruptly he reached for a book on the table as if he needed something to do with his hands. It was the erotic romance Mark had read to Scott. Craig flipped through the pages, not stopping at any one in particular, which was good considering its contents. Mark didn't want their conversation derailed. He had to figure out how to get Scott to admit the truth of what he wanted, and if Craig could help, that was just fine by him.

Craig tossed the paperback onto the table. "He doesn't want you to sacrifice something for him. He said you had a job lined up."

"I can find a different job."

But moving to Elmore? That would be hard. Too hard? Was that what Scott was thinking? That giving up Seattle was just the beginning? That he'd end up sacrificing too much one day in order to be with Scott?

"Are you two still together?"

"Yes. I asked him to stay with me."

"I don't get it." Craig sank back against the couch. He scrubbed a hand over the lower half of his face in agitation, defeat working its way through his posture. "If you're willing to go with him, and you've proven how much you care for him by not letting him walk out—because we both know that wasn't what he wanted—then why is he still not willing to admit he wants to go to that damn school?" He smacked both hands on his thighs as if at a loss for what to think, or what to do next. "I thought for sure it was about you."

"I did too." Mark studied Craig as if he could understand Scott's actions by simply observing his father, and then it hit him. "You're right. This is about him doing what he thinks is best for someone else, but it's not about me."

Craig stared at him in return, eyebrows drawn in. With that expression, those serious eyes trying to read him, he looked very much like his son. Then the confusion fled his face. "He's doing this for me."

"When he first told me why he came to school here and why he chose Michigan State for grad school, he said he didn't want to be too far from home—from you."

Craig closed his eyes as he let out a long exhale. "It appears my son and I need to have a talk." The frustration he'd had in his voice was now replaced with what sounded like concern and maybe guilt.

In the past fifteen years Mark hadn't had anyone care that much about him or what he did and why.

Until now.

Until Scott.

Craig stood. "I'm sorry I meddled again."

"It's okay." Mark followed him to the door. "I'd give anything to have my dad here to meddle in my life."

He hadn't said the words much louder than a whisper, but Craig had stopped as soon as Mark spoke. He rested a hand on Mark's shoulder and gave a squeeze.

The kindness and affection in that touch took him by surprise, had him missing his own dad more than ever. It also had him realizing how Scott had become the compassionate man he was.

Without another word, Craig gave a nod and left.

Despite knowing that both he and Craig would not give up until Scott accepted that he had to make his own decisions about his future, Mark still felt a nagging unease, like he'd made a big mistake somewhere along the way.

He didn't want to examine that too closely. He turned away from the door and went to change his clothes for the awards ceremony.

* * *

"The winner in the graphic novel category is…"

Mark drummed his fingers on his folded arms as the woman announcing the awards paused to open an envelope. From where he stood in the back of the auditorium, he couldn't see Scott, but he knew he was down in the reserved front row seats with his dad.

Scott had been given an extra ticket to invite a guest to sit with him. He had hesitated when he first opened the envelope with the tickets a week ago, so Mark hurried to suggest that Scott sit with his dad. Craig deserved to be a part of the moment.

Mark was grateful for that decision now. He was antsy and on edge where he stood in the rear of the large room, arms crossing his chest, hands gripping his biceps, waiting for the announcer to slowly, painstakingly remove the piece of paper with the winner's name.

"Could she drag this out any longer?" Owen asked from where he stood beside Mark. The impatience in his voice was a match for Mark's irritated stance.

Finally the announcer spoke again. "*The Hawk in the Caverns* by Scott Murphy."

The crowd of local faculty and students erupted in cheers, Mark and Owen joining in as they watched Scott step onto the stage. He accepted the plaque and received handshakes from the judges and the university president. Mark couldn't keep the huge grin at bay. Seemed Owen was having a similar issue.

Then out of the corner of his eye, Mark spotted a big guy in a hooded sweatshirt stalking down the side aisle.

Bruce Kreger. Looking like he was on a mission and would not stop until either someone tackled the hell out of him or he scored his goal. There was no way he was there just to watch the awards, and since he was headed for the door leading backstage that could only mean—

Mark took off. He reached him about halfway to the stage and grabbed him by the arm. "Don't even think about it. Whatever you're here to do to him, just forget it and walk away."

"Let go." Bruce jerked his arm free. "I'm not doin' nothin' to him." He continued on, and Mark gave chase until they were at the door leading backstage.

He reached around him and smacked the door shut before Bruce could get it open more than a crack. "Fine. Whatever you're here to do to me, then."

"Fuck off. Scott invited me."

"Bullshit."

The crowd was quieting down. Scott had left the stage, and the announcer was presenting the next award.

"He and I've been talkin'. Didn't he tell you?"

"Yes, he did." Not that Scott had told him about the invite. And not that Mark believed Bruce was telling him the truth anyway. He would never trust the guy, no matter what Scott thought about him.

"I was actually feelin' bad about bein' such a dick to you. Good thing Scott reminded me what an ass you are."

"What are you talking about?"

"A guy breaks up with you and you're so pathetic that you beg him to stay, then guilt him into it?"

"Are you following us again? Now who's pathetic?"

"Sure." Bruce pushed forward into Mark's space. "Because it's so easy to follow you into a closed library, on an employee-only floor, inside a locked room."

Fuck. Mark took a step back.

Bruce had to be lying. But how did he know what had happened at the library?

He couldn't have seen them, let alone heard what they'd said.

"Yeah." The arrogant son of a bitch smirked. "He told me what happened. Last time we talked online." Bruce clicked on his phone, then held it up in front of Mark's face. A Facebook conversation was on the screen.

Scott Murphy: He asked me to stay. I felt so bad. I just couldn't leave.

Bruce Kreger: He's an ass. Using guilt to fuck you over.

Scott Murphy: I think he loves me.

Bruce Kreger: If he loved you, he'd let you go. Not be a big baby about it.

Mark pointed at the phone. "That's fake."

"Sure it is. As fake as that picture you have of me on your phone."

No. Scott hadn't said that shit to Bruce; he hadn't told him anything. Mark was certain of that.

But Bruce had said one thing that was true. Mark had forced Scott into staying with him. Even if he hadn't meant to, he'd manipulated him instead of letting Scott make his own choices. Exactly the opposite of what Scott needed from him.

He'd been so wrapped up in what he was feeling for Scott, in not losing him at the end of the semester, in how damn good it had felt to finally be with someone who liked what he'd been aching to give, that he hadn't offered what Scott needed from him the most. Someone to be there, to listen, to help him become confident enough that he could find his own way in life, take the next step beyond this one competition.

Which left Mark with only one option: he had to take himself out of the equation. Scott needed to figure out what he wanted. Without thinking about anyone else.

It would just about kill him to do this, but he had to. He turned and walked out of the auditorium before he saw Scott again. He had no doubt if he got one look, he'd never be able to leave.

* * *

"Congratulations again, Mr. Murphy." The University president shook Scott's hand. "We were excited to have a student among the finalists, but to have you win was even a bigger thrill. You did the school proud."

Before Scott could get out a thank-you, the president continued on to congratulate another winner.

Scott couldn't move from where he stood beside the refreshment table at the low-key backstage gathering, clutching the wooden plaque in his hand. He wasn't so much in shock at the president's words, but at the fact that he'd actually won. It was still sinking in. He really needed to go find his dad and Owen. And Mark. That would make it more real.

"Scott Murphy?" A young man wearing a Breakout Writer Convention T-shirt was walking toward him.

"Yes."

"I need you to come with me. There's a problem with your competition entry. Someone's contesting your win."

"What?"

"The head of the awards committee will explain it to you. This way."

Scott followed him, trying not to panic as they crossed the room to a table where a middle-aged woman—who looked like she'd had to handle one too many complaints that day—sat tapping on a computer tablet propped up in front of her. She was surrounded by a slew of other conference officials.

As Scott approached she pointed to an empty chair across from her. "Have a seat."

He did so carefully, afraid the chair might slide out from under him if he moved any faster. He didn't want to make this moment worse by ending up in the emergency room with a broken ass. The look on the woman's face, and the way she was skeptically eyeing him over the tablet, told him there was no way this was going to go well for him.

"Someone has filed a complaint about your entry. Until we get this sorted out, I'm afraid your win is not official."

"Not official?" It had sure seemed official when he was standing on the stage in front of everyone. The weight of the plaque he now held on his lap definitely felt official.

"I have a few questions for you," she added.

"Okay."

"Did you plagiarize your story?"

"What? No!"

"Did you copy the drawings from something you saw online?"

"No. Is someone saying I did?"

"I'm afraid so," she said. Only she didn't seem too afraid to say that. She looked downright pissed at him. Like he'd done this on purpose to mess with her life.

Her life?

He could think of only one person who would lie about something like this, one person who would do something this malicious and callous. Yet after all they'd done to help Bruce, Scott didn't want to believe it was possible. His gut said it wasn't. How naive and foolish could he be?

"Who's saying this about me?" He needed to hear the name.

"The second-place winners." The woman pointed to two men standing off to the side, glaring at Scott. Albon and Wallace.

He wasn't sure what surprised him more—that his gut had been right about Bruce or that two total strangers would do this to him.

"So they can just make up a lie and you believe them?"

"They have proof." She spun the tablet around so he could see the screen. "This is one of their self-published stories posted online three years ago. It's available at several major websites with a publication date clearly marked. There are even reviews dating back to when the story was first published."

All that was visible was the cover. The title wasn't even remotely related to his.

"Did you look at it?" he asked.

She nodded. "The story is word for word the same as yours, and the drawings are very similar." She swiped her finger across the screen, and Scott watched in horror as page after page showed exactly what she'd said.

That couldn't be real. "I wrote Hawk's story." How could he prove it was all a lie? How did they get a copy of his book? Only the judges had seen it. And Mark.

But Mark wouldn't do anything like this to him. That wasn't even an option.

A gruff voice rang out from behind him.

"He didn't steal nothin'." Bruce stopped to stand beside him, looking more pissed than when Mark had shown him the photo of him and the bald guy on his phone. He pointed to Albon and Wallace, who did not seem at all as confident as they'd been. "They're the ones who stole his shit, and I can prove it."

Scott turned to the woman. "Could he and I have a minute to talk?"

She gave him a long stare. "Be quick. I don't want to hear what your friend has to say if he's lying in any way."

"Me either." Scott stood and moved to the far side of the backstage area, hoping Bruce got that he was supposed to follow.

When he stopped, Bruce whispered in a low, angry voice, "They're lyin'."

Scott spun to face him. "I know that. It's *my* story. But how do you know?"

Bruce hesitated, staring at the award Scott still had in his hand. He seemed reluctant to say more. Finally he gave up on the award and pointed toward the now very nervous Albon and Wallace. "Those guys broke into Mark's apartment one day when you two were gone." He pulled out his phone and swiped with his thumb for a few seconds. He showed Scott a photo of the two men at the door of Mark's apartment. They were using some kind of tool to pick the lock. "That must've been when they copied your book."

"How did you get this?"

Bruce said nothing.

"Are you still following us?"

"I wanted…" He examined the picture on his phone as if it would give him the answer. He shrugged. "I wanted to find out where that friend of Mark's lives. The one who knows places were guys go for…" He shrugged again, the movement of his shoulders more tense this time around. "You know…kinky shit. Figured he'd eventually show up at the apartment or Mark would go see him."

"You could've just asked for his name and number."

His eyebrows shot up; his jaw dropped. "Ask Mark? No way."

"He would've given it to you." Scott glanced at the picture on the phone Bruce held. "Why didn't you call the cops?"

"I didn't think they were there to mess with you. Figured they were fuckin' with Mark." He met Scott's stare, then looked away like he couldn't say the rest while keeping that contact between them. "Thought maybe he deserved whatever they were doin'."

Scott's instincts were telling him to defend Mark, but he let it go. This wasn't the right time for that discussion. "I don't know if that picture's enough proof."

Bruce scowled at him in a way he'd probably done a lot on the football field. A grin followed, transforming Bruce's face into something lighter. Softer. Almost kind.

And a little devious.

"What are you thinking?" Scott asked.

"After I saw them break in, I was curious. Followed their worthless asses, found out what their names were. Then had this girl I know look up about 'em online. They're big computer geeks like Mark. They go to a tech community college three hours south of town. Probably thought it was no trouble drivin' up here to steal your shit. She also found out they were writers and had some books out." His expression grew into something like remorse. "Guess I should've put it all together they were comin' for you. I should've warned you." He looked Scott's way, and despite his words, the devious smile returned. "She downloaded all their books to my phone that night. No way they could've drawn up their own copy to match yours by then." He searched again for something on his phone. He handed it over. "Are any of these the one they were talkin' about?"

There were only four e-books on Bruce's phone. All from Albon and Wallace.

"Yeah. This one." Scott clicked to open the file. "This isn't like my story." The book had the same cover and title as the one the woman had shown him, but the text and illustrations were completely different. "They must've copied my book and switched the file but kept the old copyright date to make it look like I stole from them."

"All 'cause they read yours and knew you was a shoo-in to win."

"Can I borrow this?" He indicated the phone.

"Go for it."

Scott faced the table where the woman and the other officials sat waiting, watching him. He'd never had to do anything like this. He was probably going to ruin Albon's and Wallace's writing careers. But what had Mark said about Bruce? Didn't the same apply here? They'd made their own beds. They chose to concoct this ridiculous lie.

He took a deep breath and headed for the table, silently repeating one line over and over again, confidence building with each step he took.

* * *

"Bruce!" Scott jogged down the hallway leading away from the backstage area. "Wait up." He held off on saying more until he caught up with him. "They came clean. Said they'd lied about the plagiarism and copied my book to back up their claims."

"I heard."

"It's official now. I won."

Bruce gave a nod that Scott knew was meant as congratulations. The pleased look on Bruce's face painted him in a much more attractive light than any of his previous expressions. There was something very sexy about that thin smile that just barely tugged at the corners of his lips. When he found the courage to hit a gay bar, he was going to be very popular.

Scott handed him his phone. "Thanks for helping me out back there. I don't know what I would've done if you hadn't told me about the break-in and showed me their books."

"You'd have figured somethin' out."

"I sounded stupid trying to explain it all."

"Nah. You sounded smart to me." He turned away, like he didn't want to say what had just crossed his mind. Then without another word, he started down the hall.

"I thought it was you," Scott called after him.

Bruce stopped.

"When she first told me someone said I'd plagiarized, I thought it was you messing with me."

"Yeah," he drawled. He faced Scott, his lips turned up in an even more amused smirk than before. That had his eyes lighting up. They were a brilliant blue. Scott had never noticed that before.

He was definitely going to be real popular with guys.

"A few weeks ago," Bruce added, his tone tinged with humor like he couldn't believe he was admitting this, "I probably would've paid those guys to do it."

"I'm still sorry I thought that about you."

He slid his hands in the pockets of his sweatshirt. "Forget it." He took off down the hall again.

"Why did you come here today? It wasn't to watch the awards, was it?"

Without facing Scott, Bruce sighed; his shoulders slumped. He seemed smaller in that moment, less imposing. "I wanted to break you two up. I wanted him to lose what he cared about most. Just like I did."

"You tried that before with his dissertation." Scott chuckled at that, trying to ease the tension, despite the truth in his words. "You gotta come up with some new ideas."

"Never said I was as smart as you." Bruce laughed too, but Scott didn't join him that time.

Instead he stepped closer so he was standing beside him. "You want to get together for lunch sometime?"

Bruce hesitated, scrutinizing Scott like he'd find some ulterior motive if he looked hard enough.

It must suck not to trust anyone like that. Even when Scott hadn't had many friends in school, he always had his dad. He was certain it was that consistency of love and safety that had kept him from learning to mistrust everyone. Some people weren't that lucky.

"I could help you," he told Bruce.

"With what?"

"Learn how to read."

That had Bruce glaring at him, but he didn't deny it.

Scott was fairly sure Mark was going to hate this, but he had to do what felt right.

With that realization came another truth that slammed into him like a jab in the gut. He hadn't been doing what felt right. Not when it came to grad school or his dad.

Or Mark.

Chapter Ten

"Fuck that. I can read."

Bruce's outraged tone had Scott pushing aside the regret about his recent choices.

Bruce kept scowling at him from where he leaned against the narrow hall's opposite wall.

"But you can't read all that well, right? That's why you have to pay people to do your homework for you, and why you had to get someone to help you research those guys online. It's why you didn't know if the book that woman mentioned was on your phone." He paused, not wanting to hurt Bruce's feelings, but he needed to say the last bit. "And it's why you're such a jerk to smart guys like me."

Bruce shook his head, but in contrast to that he said, "If you tell anyone—"

"I won't. I've got a little time before the semester ends, and I'd like to help you."

"Why?"

"Everyone should know how to read. Reading saved me when I was that weird, geeky kid in school no one wanted to talk to."

"Are you going to start singin' some lame-ass song about books bein' your best friend?"

He laughed. "No." He could've gone on and on about books being his friends growing up, but he held back. Bruce had gotten his point. "But you know, you're not going to get a college degree, at least not from this school, and without being able to read, it might be tough getting a job." He waited a moment, but Bruce said nothing, which probably meant he hadn't come up with a plan for what he'd do next. "You said you didn't want to disappoint your dad. You don't have to be the same man he is to impress him, but you do have to live the best life you can, be the best man you can be. If that doesn't impress him, then he's not worth worrying about."

Bruce rolled his eyes, the action laced with amusement. "You're pretty fuckin' smart, you know that?" He leaned his head back against the wall behind him and breathed deep. "God, I'm tired. Of everything." Then he straightened suddenly, like he had to take off just to get away from his own feelings. He turned to leave but halted before taking a step away. "You think we could start tomorrow?"

"Yeah. Meet me at Not Just Java at ten. I'll bring the number for Mark's friend too. So you can find out about those places to meet guys." Scott started off down the hall toward the auditorium. "I gotta get going." His dad and Owen and Mark were waiting for him.

"Hey, you'll have to go find Mark. He left."

That had Scott faltering on his next step. "Left?"

"What can I say? The guy's an asshole." Bruce held up a hand before Scott could say anything. "Guess he's your asshole, though."

"He is. I mean—"

"I get it. When you find him, tell him I paid a guy in campus security to let me watch the cameras in the library, and that he's the one who faked the Facebook chat for me too. And tell him... Tell him I'm sorry about all that." He waved his hand through the air. "He'll know what I mean."

"Okay. See you tomorrow." Scott wasn't sure what Bruce was talking about, but he had to find Mark, had to explain a few things and apologize for trying to break up with him. He headed for the stage area, then went out into the auditorium. Except for a few stragglers, the room had pretty much cleared out now that the awards were over. He found Owen and his dad sitting in the front row talking.

Owen stood when he spotted him. "Hey! Congratulations." He held out a hand, and when they shook, he pulled Scott close and patted his back.

Then Scott's dad gave him a long hug. "I'm so proud of you, kiddo."

"Thanks."

"So," Owen said, "when will we get to buy a copy in bookstores?"

"An editor with the publishing house has to look at it first, decide if they want to publish it."

"They will." Owen gave a squeeze to his shoulder that time. "I gotta get back to the coffee shop. You guys stop by later. Cake is on me. All you can eat." He winked Scott's way.

"Thanks, Owen. For everything."

As Owen headed down the center aisle, Scott scanned the rest of the auditorium, hoping that Mark had come back.

"He was here earlier," his dad said.

"It's weird that he left. I really need to talk to him. Do you think we could postpone our dinner, maybe celebrate another day?"

"Sure. But you and I need to have a talk first." He gestured to two chairs in the front row. "It'll just take a few minutes."

"Oh, okay." Scott sat in one of the chairs, not at all liking the serious resolve with which his dad had spoken. He'd only heard him sound like that a handful of times. Usually it meant that Scott had done something wrong and had let his dad down. There was nothing that ever felt as bad as that, so he'd always done all he could to avoid having that disappointment directed at him. "What's wrong?"

"You."

"Me?"

His dad took a seat beside him, worry etched on his face. "You need to go to that school in New York. I know it's what you want to do."

"I'm not sure—"

"I know the reason you're not going has nothing to do with you. And it's really not even about Mark. It's about me."

Scott couldn't deny that. He couldn't lie to his dad.

"Just because your mother died during childbirth, that does not mean you are to blame, and it does not mean you owe me anything."

"I know that." In theory, he did.

"Your mother would have done everything exactly the same way, even if she knew how her life would end. She would never have blamed you. Which means you can't blame yourself. She'd want you to live your own life. You owe her that."

Tears burned at the corners of Scott's eyes. He nodded.

His dad slid an arm around his shoulders and gave him a one-arm hug. He kissed him on the top of the head before letting go. His next words shot through the air like he had to get them out before he changed his mind.

"I'm dating someone." He wouldn't make eye contact with Scott. He stared at his palms resting in his lap, looking incredibly nervous, which was not usual for him. "I've been seeing her since you first left for college four years ago. And she's not the first woman I've been involved with since your mother's death. I never wanted you to know about any of them until I was ready to get married again, until I found someone I wanted to spend the rest of my life with. I didn't want you to get attached and then lose her like I lost your mother."

Scott stared at his dad's profile. He wasn't sure what to think.

There was an entire part of his dad's life he knew nothing about, that he'd hidden from him.

Before he could think of what to say, his dad continued, looking more sure of what he was saying.

"I still believe that was the right call when you were little, but perhaps I kept that rule going too long. I think I've given you the impression that I have no one in my life other than you. That I have no friends, no lovers. I made our lives about you and forgot to show you that I do have other people to spend time with. That I don't need you to take care of me. At least not yet. Maybe someday when I keep forgetting where I left my teeth." He smiled around a laugh.

That had Scott feeling more at ease. This was still his dad, after all. The man who raised him and taught him to love books and reading, and taught him about the kind of man he wanted to be.

"I wish you would've told me."

"I know. I'm sorry about that. Renee struggled through an ugly marriage and an even uglier divorce. I knew it would be quite a while before she was ready to get married again. I had it in my head that getting engaged was when I should tell you. That was what I'd promised myself when you were a baby. But now… Renee is a wonderful person, and I'd really like you to meet her."

"I'd like that too."

"Maybe then you'll see that I'm fine, and I'll be fine while you're in New York. You and I will always have a relationship. We'll always stay in touch no matter where you are."

"I know." He paused, letting his dad's words wash away the promises he'd made himself when he first went to college. "I want to accept the fellowship."

His dad watched him, said nothing. He was waiting for more.

"I'm going to accept it."

* * *

Mark sat at a table staring at the comic books spread out before him. He still wore the dress shirt and tie he'd had on at the awards ceremony. The library was closed, and he was alone in one of the study rooms. The same room where he'd first had sex with Scott.

After he'd left the competition, he got a message from his boss that the additional shelving display units she'd ordered had come in and that she'd appreciate it if he worked on them this weekend. He'd decided assembling shelves was a much better way to keep busy than staring at his apartment ceiling. The task would give him something to focus on other than how he'd walked out on Scott's big moment.

And yet, he hadn't even opened the boxes. He'd gone straight for the comic collection and pulled out binder after binder of superhero comics. He'd taken the stack of binders to the study room and laid them out on the table before him where he scanned through each book, thinking about what made a man a hero, trying to find the answers to questions he thought he'd long ago come to understand about his life and his future.

Thinking about Scott.

A half hour later, he still sat staring at the comics, feeling like the villain of every one of those stories. Walking away might've been the right move for Scott, but Mark had taken the coward's way out with how he did it.

He had to talk to him. Had to apologize. He also had to explain that Scott was right the other day. This had to end. It was time for Scott to figure out on his own what he truly wanted out of his life, without Mark there messing with his head, dominating him when he needed the exact opposite.

Mark dug his phone out of his pocket and opened a new text message. He'd never been at such a loss for words. If he didn't send the text, he could just sit there surrounded by the slew of comics and pretend he and Scott weren't ending.

His thumb hovered over the phone.

It dinged with a new text message. Meet me where we first kissed.

He wasn't sure how Scott planned to get into the elevator, let alone the closed library, but it didn't matter.

He sent back: On my way.

He went out into the hall and waited. The elevator was on its way up. As each floor number lit up overhead, the unease slipped further and further away. He felt more in control, more sure of what he wanted, despite what he'd been telling himself just minutes before.

The elevator doors opened. Scott was leaning against the back wall, like the first time Mark had stood in that same spot watching him. Only this time Scott's eyes weren't closed. He was staring back at him.

The elevator started to close. Mark lifted an arm to stop the doors. "Get over here." His dominant side sliding into place, he returned to that comfortable ease where he could just be himself, like he always felt around Scott. Which, yet again, went against everything he'd been trying to convince himself of since he talked to Bruce earlier.

Scott stepped forward without delay.

"How did you know I was up here?" Mark asked.

"I heard the message from your boss at your apartment."

"How did you get inside?"

"I called her. She met me and let me in."

"Why would she do that?"

"I told her the reason I needed to talk to you. I think she's a fan of romances. This has all the makings of a big romantic ending."

Mark raised his eyebrows. "It does?"

"Yeah."

When Scott didn't offer more, Mark held up his phone. "I was just about to text you."

"What were you going to say?"

"I don't know. Something."

Scott reached for the phone. He typed and handed it back. "Try this."

I'm sorry I took off. I was...

"Now you fill in the blank."

Mark took a step back, knowing he had to keep some distance or he'd reach out and touch Scott. "I was avoiding this conversation."

"Which one? The one where I tell you about how someone failed at getting me disqualified for plagiarism? Or the one where I promised I'd teach Bruce to read? Or the one where Bruce told me some cryptic message for you about a security guard letting him watch the cameras at the library and a faked Facebook chat?"

"How long ago did I leave that auditorium?"

"It was a busy day." Scott moved in closer, shrinking the distance between them to less than it had been a moment ago. "I wish you had been there."

"I saw you win."

"Yeah?"

Mark couldn't stop himself. He reached out and took Scott's hand in his, gave it a squeeze. "I'm really proud of you."

They stood there, the two of them connected by the simple touch of their hands, and Mark wanted to say fuck doing the right thing and instead take Scott to the study room so they could really celebrate his win. He forced himself to remain motionless.

Scott rubbed his thumb over the backs of Mark's fingers. "I always imagined you'd kiss me right after I won."

Again Mark held still, going against every instinct he'd always had when it came to Scott. "I want you to know, I didn't leave today because of what Bruce told me."

"I don't even know what he said."

"It doesn't matter. I knew he was lying. Was it Bruce who said you'd plagiarized?"

"No. It was the guys who placed second. Guess they were pretty desperate to get a shot at a publishing contract. Bruce helped me prove they were lying. I had to explain it to the woman in charge of the event. I was scared she wouldn't believe me. All these people were there watching me talk to her."

That took Mark back to their first night together when Scott had said he could never teach because he didn't like people watching him, listening to him.

"I'm sure you did great."

"My knees were shaking. Then I remembered what you said. I kept repeating it to myself over and over."

"What did I say?"

"Love makes you brave." He came in close, slipped a hand around the back of Mark's neck, and drew him down. It was a long, sweet press of their mouths. Scott's lips parted under his, and when Scott's tongue slid into the kiss, Mark nearly lost all his resolve to think things through instead of letting his desires and emotions take over.

Slowly Scott pulled back, their combined hands never letting go. "I'm going to accept the fellowship in New York."

"You should."

"I want you to come with me. If the offer still stands. I'll understand if Seattle's where you need to be, but maybe we could keep seeing each other. I just…" He raised their clasped hands and held on tighter, like he wanted to keep that one connection going as long as he could. "I don't want to lose this."

"Me either, but I think…" Mark's next move was one of the hardest things he'd ever done. He let go of Scott and walked past him along the length of the glass windows outside the popular culture rooms, a part of him desperately begging himself to stop this before he said the words. He stood at a window that featured a display of vintage movie postcards. One was of Christopher Reeve as Superman. The large black text read *Man of Steel*. "I think maybe you need to do this on your own. Without your dad there. Without me there. Where every decision you make is all about you." He let out a shaky breath.

Scott came to stand beside him. He reached up and ran the tip of his index finger over the glass like he was tracing the image of Superman. Finally he said, "I don't want to be the kind of person who makes decisions that are always all about me."

"And that's why I think you were right before. We need to end this." He couldn't force himself to turn toward Scott, didn't want to see his reaction. At least when Scott had tried to break up with him, he did it face-to-face. So much for the big romantic ending. Mark was no hero. He couldn't even call it quits in an admirable way. He stepped away and stopped at the display in the next window, his back to Scott.

"Volintium." The one word that came from behind him was soft but spoken with complete conviction.

He spun around. "What?"

"You told me to use my safe word if you ever did something I didn't want. You're walking away from us, and I don't want that."

"That's not..." Mark shook his head. "I don't want to mess up your life."

"How are you messing it up?"

"I'm influencing what you think and feel."

"That's what happens in a relationship."

"It's different for you. You don't want to disappoint or hurt anyone. I think you need to find your own way before you get into a long-term relationship, before you fall in love with someone."

"Well"—Scott took a step closer—"it's too late for that. I've been in love with you for a while now. And I'm doing exactly what I want. I'm telling you what I want. You're the one who's doing what you think is best instead of listening to me. Instead of doing what you know we both want you to do."

Mark studied him. The wisdom of Scott's words took him aback. Somehow he'd managed to miss that Scott was telling him both what he wanted to hear and what he needed to hear. Scott had tracked him down and was using his safe word because he was brave enough to put his heart on the line, just like he'd been brave enough to put his story in the competition. "You're pretty smart. And a hell of a lot stronger than I've been giving you credit for."

Scott smiled, but it was a forced expression. He was trembling. That about-to-panic look had Mark's earlier instincts kicking into gear.

Love makes you brave.

He held out his arms. "Come here."

Scott stepped into the embrace, and in that moment, Mark had no other choice. He tipped Scott's head back so they were looking at each other. "New York, huh?"

"Yeah. I have to go."

"Yeah, you do." *Love makes you brave.* "I can definitely do New York."

"What about after? I might still want to move home."

"I don't know. But we'll have lots of time to talk about it."

"Like couples do."

"Right." How had he been so stupid? If they moved to Elmore, and he absolutely hated it, they'd talk about it, work things out together. Besides, he'd need to have a job somewhere. There were several colleges within driving distance, in larger cities where they could even live and still be near Elmore. They'd figure it out.

He said, "I'm sorry I tried to push you away. When I didn't think you were making the choices you wanted—"

"But I am now."

"Your dad talked to you?"

"Yeah. I think I've figured out how to tell people what I want." With both hands he reached up and held Mark's face. He ran the pads of his thumbs over his lips, tracing them like he'd done with the image of Superman. "I want to be with you. However we have to make that work for both of us. I want you to keep taking me to that place where I can just be and feel and not think so much. I want you to be yourself and show me everything you've ever wanted but had no one to go there with."

Mark exhaled a long sigh of amazement, letting the last of his worry and fears disappear. He kissed Scott, offering everything he had to give—his thanks and agreement and affection—in that one kiss.

When they parted Scott buried his face at the base of Mark's throat and held him.

Mark returned the embrace. "I've been running away from things for too long. No matter what I do, where I go, my dad will still be gone, my brothers will still be assholes, and I'll still want to be with you, Scott, wherever we end up."

Scott sucked in a quick breath. The same way he did when Mark had first touched him, when he'd first spanked him in that study room. Then he tilted his head back, and they kissed again. It wasn't about dominance or submission. It wasn't a kiss leading to something more. It was a tender affirmation of what they'd both confessed.

Mark wanted it to go on and on. Then a thought hit him. "You're teaching Bruce to read?"

"Oh, yeah. I wasn't sure you heard that part."

"I still don't trust that guy."

"You don't have to, but this is something I have to do."

"I know." He paused, ran a hand down Scott's back. "You changed his life."

"Bruce's?"

"He was such an ass that he alienated anyone who could've helped him accept himself. But you helped him anyway."

Scott said nothing, but he held on a little tighter.

"So," Mark started again, switching to a more controlled voice, "what are you doing tonight?"

Those wide, trusting eyes staring up at him were begging him for more of what they'd first done in the library. "Whatever you tell me to."

Mark hesitated. He wanted so badly to fall into the moment with Scott, wanted to believe what Scott had said about his desire to go to this place with him, not to worry if this was what he needed from him—he wanted to trust Scott. But could he?

"Don't." Scott forced him to look him in the eyes. "You can do this. It's what we both want. When you give this to me, when I let you lead the way, it makes me feel stronger, like I can do anything. And in the middle of it, I know there's nothing you wouldn't do for me. It's powerful, and I feel closer to you than anyone who's ever touched me." He let go of him and sank to his knees, his palms brushing the outsides of Mark's legs all the way down to his shins. Once again that wide, trusting gaze was locked on Mark's. "Please."

That deliberate move, the whispered beg, wiped away the last of Mark's doubt. Scott was learning to voice his desires, to admit to what he wanted, yet still embrace who he was, to give into this side of himself, and to trust Mark. He deserved for Mark to give him the same trust.

He cupped Scott's cheek. "Not here. There are cameras. Go into the study room, stand against the far wall, and wait for me."

Slowly, with obvious relief, Scott lowered his eyelids and nodded. He turned his head and pressed his parted lips against Mark's thumb.

The warm breaths hitting the pad of his thumb were almost as exquisite as the whispered words that followed.

"I love you."

Then Scott was on his feet, rushing for the study room.

Mark watched his retreat—his beautiful surrender to him—and he knew...

This was it.

He had always wondered how people knew when they'd found that one person they wanted to spend the rest of their lives with. Even with the high divorce rate, it amazed him that so many couples did work out—that one day they just decided to get married, and then spent forty, fifty, sixty years together. How had they known that early on that this person was the one for them?

Now he got it.

Completely, unequivocally he understood how a person knew such a thing.

He followed him into the popular culture library and started down the hall for the comics room. He was divided between taking his time to give Scott a chance to anticipate what would come next and rushing to the room so Scott didn't end up worried that he might not be coming.

The latter won out.

Inside the room, he closed the door behind him. Scott was standing with his back against the wall. The table covered in comics divided the space between them. Mark rounded it and went to him, bracing his hands against the wall on either side of Scott's shoulders. He leaned down to kiss the side of his neck, his lips and tongue tracing an invisible path up his skin that had Scott's breath hitching again.

He hovered his lips over Scott's ear, letting him hear his own ragged breaths, pressing their bodies together so Scott could feel his erection, feel how much he wanted him like this. He waited another moment, then whispered, "I love you too."

He didn't want Scott to doubt that. Not now. Not ever.

Scott reached out and gripped Mark's forearm like he needed the contact to steady himself, like he'd waited his whole life to hear those words.

Mark held him by the back of the head so they were pressed temple to temple. "Are you okay?"

Scott nodded, gripped him tighter, then drew in a deep breath and let go. "Yes." He returned his hands to the wall beside him on both sides.

"Are you sure?" Mark asked. "We can wait—"

"No! Please." Scott licked his lips, and the desire was clear in his eyes, in every part of him. "Please."

That was enough for Mark. Hands on Scott's shoulders, he gave a slight shove, and Scott was on his knees again. "Clasp your hands behind your back. Open my pants."

Scott gave him a questioning look.

Mark ran the back of his index finger over Scott's lips. "With your teeth."

Scott leaned in and pinched the fabric on one side of the button between his teeth and tugged. He got the zipper halfway down, then was sidetracked nuzzling Mark's dick with his mouth, wetting the fabric like he couldn't wait to get it out of the way.

"Shit." Mark grabbed a fistful of his hair and forced him to back off for a moment. He tore open his own pants, slid the briefs down just enough to get his dick out, and then guided Scott back to him. "Stick out your tongue." He gripped his cock and tapped the tip against Scott's lips and tongue again and again, loving the vibrations that surged along his shaft with each contact, loving even more the way Scott looked right then. His hair mussed, hands clasped behind his back, gaze glued to Mark's, his lips wet, his hungry mouth open, eager.

Mark wanted to feed that mouth his cock, but he had an even better idea.

He took a step back. Then another, slowly backing away, letting the power of the movement flow through him, allowing the dominant side of him to have full access. He pulled a chair out from the table. He sat, slouched a bit, spread his legs. His cock hung free from the opening in the front of his pants.

He rested his hands on each side of his groin, close to his dick but not touching it. "Stand up. Remove your shirt."

Scott did as he was told, moving swiftly to undo the buttons on his dress shirt.

"Slow down. We've got all night." They had a lot of nights to come. Years. "Now your pants."

He watched as Scott stripped off the rest of his clothes, one article at a time. When he was naked, Mark said, "Come here."

Scott stood before him, his dick moist at the tip. Mark was pretty sure if he took him in his mouth right then, Scott would explode on contact. Knowing that just undressing for him had Scott this ready to pop was intoxicating.

He gripped the base of Scott's dick and squeezed. "Breathe. Deep breaths."

Scott closed his eyes and drew air into his lungs.

"Look at me." Mark deliberately, slowly stroked him, gathering the moisture at the tip with his thumb and spreading it around, hitting the sensitive skin beneath the head of his dick with each swipe.

That had Scott's lips parting. He sucked in a sharp breath, but he didn't look away.

"Scott Murphy." Mark paused for effect, then spoke again using the steady, low voice that he knew drove Scott crazy. "You are mine. You know that?"

"Yes." Scott's hips moved as Mark worked him faster. "I'm yours."

"Straddle me."

He let him go so Scott could arrange himself, facing him. He loved being naked with Scott, but this—still fully clothed, only his dick exposed, with Scott naked and touching him—always fed something primal in him.

He grasped Scott's wrists and held them in one hand behind Scott's back. With his other hand he undid his tie and slipped it off. Once he had Scott's hands secured behind his back, he leaned in and flicked one of Scott's nipples with his tongue, sucked on it, making love to that one hard point.

That had Scott writhing, tugging on the hold of the tie. Not enough to get loose, because they both knew he didn't want that.

Mark sat up and held out a hand, palm up. "Spit."

Scott leaned down, never looking away from him. He always seemed to need that option of being able to meet Mark's gaze. He needed that connection, and that was just fine by Mark.

He could read a lot in those expressive eyes.

Scott wet his lips and let saliva drip from his mouth to Mark's hand.

Something about the complete lewdness of that action had Mark's dick aching even more. He ran his hand over his own cock, wetting it, dying to keep stroking. He was that close to the edge already. He forced himself to let go and held out his hand again. "More."

Scott repeated the action, and Mark ran his wet palm over Scott's dick that time, encouraging him to slide closer while he kept on stroking.

He angled his own hips until their cocks were lined up. He grasped them both so he was pumping them together with two hands. With Scott on top of him, the tip of Mark's dick only reached halfway up Scott's length, but that was almost better. After his hands moved up their erections on each stroke, he focused the last bit solely on the head of Scott's dick, spreading the saliva around and pressing his thumb to the slit.

Now Scott had his eyes closed. "Oh God. Please."

That beg sounded more intense, more meaningful than the ones Mark had first heard in the same library, that same room. He jerked them faster.

Scott threw his head back and rocked into the touches.

That additional friction of their erections sliding together sent another intense sensation coursing through Mark.

"Scott."

At hearing his name, he met Mark's gaze.

"Lean forward. Open your mouth."

With his hands still secured behind his back, Scott dropped his head and parted his lips. Mark kept stroking, faster, uncontrollably bucking up against Scott's spread thighs. He grunted and came, his release shooting up toward Scott. The first small spurt landed on Scott's chin, but the rest hit his lips and tongue.

Despite the fact that Mark had slowed the movement of his hand on Scott to a tender swipe of his palm, Scott started coming as soon as his tongue licked the cum from his lips. Mark quickened his hand and helped Scott through the last of his body's trembling release.

When he finally stilled, Scott slumped against him. "Oh God. Thank you."

Several moments went by as Mark's rapid heartbeat slowed, and only then did Scott's words register. "Thank *me*?" They hadn't even fucked. He freed Scott's wrists and tugged him closer, adjusting his own ass on the chair to avoid sending them sliding off onto the floor. "I didn't even get to bend you over the table like that first time we were in here."

Scott braced himself on Mark's shoulders and sat up, his eyebrows drawn in, head cocked to the side, displaying that curious, confused expression Mark had first loved about him. "This meant a thousand times more to me than that day."

"Yeah. For me too."

When Scott gave him a smile, Mark pulled him close and held him again.

The quiet of the empty library around them seemed fitting. Just the two of them, and rows and rows of books.

Yet none of the people in those books, real or imagined—not even the ones in the superhero comics sitting on the table beside them— came close to the incredible, brave man in his arms.

Seattle. New York. Elmore, Michigan. No matter where they were, they'd have each other. That was more than enough for him.

And of course, there was always the public library.

Epilogue

"Some of these look like giant penises."

Scott felt his face flush the moment the words left his mouth. But he couldn't have been the first person to think that about the stalactites and stalagmites that filled the Ohio Valley Caverns.

Mark chuckled from behind him.

Oddly that had Scott feeling more at ease, not embarrassed.

They'd been hiking for forty-five minutes through the winding tunnels that led one hundred feet below surface. The two-hundred-thousand-year-old white crystals stood out beautifully against the colorful walls of the caverns. Browns and oranges, reds and blues. The path was narrow in some places, the cave walls on each side close enough to touch. The air around them felt cool and crisp.

At several points along the tour, the walls opened up to larger caves. Mark had secured them a private guide who explained about the formation of the caverns and offered facts on the array of crystal formations within. Usually visitors followed the lit, marked path, wearing headphones with a recorded message about the caverns. That Mark had thought to bring Scott for a private tour where he could ask questions was just the coolest thing anyone had ever done for him.

After Mark had passed his dissertation defense, he said he wanted to do something special for both of them. They'd gone for a celebratory dinner that night with Scott's dad and Renee, and then Mark had surprised him with the tickets for the tour.

At first, while the guide had talked, Scott had held back on asking too much, but how often would he get the chance to talk to someone this knowledgeable about the caverns? So he'd spent the last thirty minutes of the tour asking question after question that clearly no guest had ever known enough to ask and had the guide as excited as Scott.

When they'd reached the large room with the penis-shaped formations, the guide answered Scott's last question and then excused himself. Apparently included in the purchase of their private tour was some time alone in the largest cave. Scott wanted to explore every inch of it. There was a main path that wound around the perimeter of the room and then branched off into more paths that circled the larger formations coming up out of the floor.

"How long can we stay here?" he asked.

Mark meandered along the path toward him. "We've got time. A lot of time, actually. Next tour's not for two hours. I paid extra so we could be alone." He was looking at Scott with that same intensity he'd directed at him since they arrived at the caverns, like he wanted to devour him. It was hard to miss, even with the more than fifteen feet, mounds of rock, and all sizes of stalagmites separating them. "I didn't want you to miss anything." He gestured with an arm toward the rest of the room. "What do you think?"

"I didn't know the rocks would be so red and golden." Scott took out his phone from his backpack and made sure the flash was on. He snapped a series of photos, then traded the phone for a notepad and a pen and took down some notes. He'd already started writing the next book in his series but hadn't drawn anything for it yet. Now he'd be able to incorporate more details and enhancements this time around, things he didn't think to add without having seen the caverns firsthand.

He walked along the main walkway toward the far side of the room, checking the width of the path as he went. It was the same as the smallest of the ones they'd followed earlier.

"I think I made the dragons just the right size. Any larger and they wouldn't have been able to turn around down here."

He spotted a small alcove about ten feet to his left, near the base of the wall. He moved in closer. Before reaching it, he spied another, even larger opening that had been hidden in the shadows. This one was about four feet tall. Only it wasn't an alcove. It was an entranceway to another cave. A rope was tied across the opening with a sign that read *No public access allowed.*

He used his phone's display to shine a light into the opening, but he couldn't see all that far. He moved on to the second alcove. There was something shiny lying on the floor. A small, flat box covered in silver paper that glinted in the light.

"There's something in here."

Mark headed toward him, a look of concern on his face. "Be careful."

"It's okay. I think someone must've lost it." Scott reached for the box. It wasn't heavy. The paper on the outside was sparkling wrapping paper, and taped on the front was a handwritten note that read *Congratulations, Scott!*

He stood and faced Mark. Only he wasn't there.

"Mark?"

No answer.

He glanced around the cave, found nothing.

The rope in the opening he'd spotted earlier now hung unsecured on one side. "Mark?"

Still no answer. A light came on inside the second cave, then another light until the golden rock walls and roof of the opening were cast in a soft glow.

Scott ducked his head and went through the opening. He could stand upright once inside the room. It was much smaller than any of the other caves. Cozy. Intimate. There were two chairs, a table, and several small battery-powered lanterns set up inside. Mark stood beside the table.

"Are we allowed in here?"

He nodded. "It's part of the private time I paid for."

Scott pointed to the table. "Is that too?"

"Yes."

He moved closer. A box marked with the logo for Not Just Java sat on the table beside two plates and forks. Through the clear top of the box he could see the chocolate cake inside. White icing spelled out the words *Congratulations, Mark and Scott.* The words were written above a black plastic graduation cap with a gold tassel. The top of the table was scratched and covered in handwritten names and notes. One message stood out: *For a good time call Carly.*

"This is the table from the library. The table where we—" Scott reached out and ran the tips of his fingers over the words carved into the surface.

Mark moved in behind him and pressed against his back. "Where we first fucked."

"How did you…?"

"The library bought new tables for all the study rooms. They were just going to throw this out. I saved it, drove down here yesterday, and planned out this little surprise with the guy who runs the caverns. Told him how tomorrow we are graduating and then leaving for New York, and that I wanted our last night to be special. He was hesitant, but his wife overheard us. She said it was the most romantic thing she'd ever heard of, even more than the endings of all those romance novels she reads." He whispered his next words against Scott's ear. "You didn't open your present."

Scott still had the shiny silver box in his hand.

Mark turned him until they faced each other. "Go on."

Scott tore open the paper. A copy of *My Side of the Mountain* lay inside. "You remembered." He opened it. A first edition. "This is too much."

"No, it's not. Besides, it wasn't expensive. Just hard to find. Someone my mom knows who has a bookstore in Chicago tracked down a copy for me."

Scott turned the pages, remembering why he'd fallen in love with this book as a child. And why he'd fallen for the man standing before him. "This makes my gift for you seem lame."

"I already got what I wanted." Mark settled a hand on Scott's lower back and tugged him forward. "More than I'd thought possible."

That deep voice and the commanding action had Scott slipping into that safe place that came to him whenever Mark took control of the moment. It gave him the courage to slide off his backpack and tug out the long, thin envelope. "I didn't get a chance to wrap it." He handed it over, not even sure he'd been this nervous sending *The Hawk in the Caverns* to the competition, or waiting in the auditorium to hear if he'd won the award.

Mark removed the comic. *The Librarian in the Stacks*. "Oh man."

"This one's just for you." Scott wasn't sure he could ever publish anything that erotic. Let alone one that was clearly about him and Mark and their love of bondage.

On the cover were two men leaning against a shelving unit full of books. They were kissing, both shirtless, their bodies pressed together. The taller man still had a tie around his neck. It hung down over his bare chest. A black tie with a splash of red zigzagging across the front. The other had a backpack at his feet.

Mark turned to the first page, and his eyes widened. "This is about when we met."

"Yeah. Sorry it won't be an exciting read. I mean, you already know how it ends."

"Well, then, I know it's going to be really damn good."

"Are you sure?" He wasn't asking about their past. He was asking about where they'd go from here. One look, and he knew Mark got that.

"I'm positive."

Under the golden lamplight bouncing off the cave walls, Mark's strong face and the warm, devoted look in those dark eyes had Scott wanting to sketch a drawing of him. Because no matter what Mark said about who the hero was where Bruce was concerned, Scott had the inspiration for the hero of his new book. Mark fit the bill perfectly.

Mark turned another page of the comic. "Damn." He must have hit one of the sex scenes. "We look good together. Is this how you see me?"

Scott nodded, finding it hard to speak, slipping further into that zone where he wanted Mark to make him feel needed and used and special.

Mark flipped through more pages. He laughed. "I like how you drew Bruce. All Jekyll and Hyde.

"He just looks normal in the end."

Mark met his stare. "Because the hero of the story saved him. *You* saved him."

"Is that really how you see me?"

"It is."

"Most people think I'm a weak book geek."

Mark set the comic on the table behind Scott. He held him by the back of the neck and leaned down so they were eye level. "Then they weren't really looking. It's not just how I see you. It's who you are." He turned him around so Scott was nestled back against Mark's strong body. He reached for the table and picked up a black napkin. Only it wasn't a napkin. It was a long black tie. He handed it to Scott. "Blindfold yourself."

Scott covered his eyes, knotting the fabric behind his head.

Mark kissed below his earlobe and whispered, "Be quiet. Breathe it in. Feel it."

He wasn't sure what Mark meant by that, but he tilted his head back to rest against Mark's shoulder. Their combined breaths were the only sounds in the underground world. He breathed deep. The crisp air was invigorating and smelled of damp earth and rock but seemed somehow cleaner than the air above ground, untouched by pollution and debris. Mark raised Scott's arm and ran his open hand over the rock wall beside them. Scott's fingers brushed the smooth, rounded ribbons of cool limestone. With his eyes covered, every texture, every curved ridge stood out.

Mark kept their hands moving, helping him explore the surface. Scott felt connected to the caverns—more aware of his surroundings and its beauty than merely looking at it had offered. That Mark had thought to help him experience this meant more to him than anything else they'd done together in or out of bed.

Mark cupped his chin and turned his head to the side. "You were the best part of college for me. You taught me more than anything or anyone else." He brushed his lips against Scott's. "Thank you for trusting me, for loving me."

With those words, with that one touch, Scott knew—no matter how great it was to get lost in a story, his real life had somehow turned out much better than any book.

AUTHOR'S NOTE

MORE THAN JUST A GOOD BOOK includes brief excerpts from my novel *MORE*, a gay menage erotic romance originally published in e-book format by Loose Id, LLC in 2010. Learn more about *MORE* and my other titles at www.sloanparker.com.

Sloan Parker

OTHER TITLES BY SLOAN PARKER

More
Breathe
Take Me Home
How to Save a Life (The Haven #1)
The Break-In
Swept Away
Something to Believe In

ABOUT THE AUTHOR

Sloan Parker writes passionate, dramatic stories about two men (or more) falling in love. She enjoys writing in the fictional world because in fiction you can be anything, do anything—even fall in love for the first time over and over again. Sloan lives in Ohio with her partner and their neurotic cats. Her greatest moments in life are spent with her family, her friends, and her characters.

To contact Sloan, find out about her other books that are available for purchase, and read free stories, visit: www.sloanparker.com. If you'd like to be notified of new releases and get exclusive sneak peeks, be sure to sign up to receive Sloan Parker's newsletter via her website.